Nina Mathias is a Civil S

NINA MATHIAS

The Molehill

GRAFTON BOOKS
A Division of the Collins Publishing Group

LONDON GLASGOW
TORONTO SYDNEY AUCKLAND

Grafton Books
A Division of the Collins Publishing Group
8 Grafton Street, London W1X 3LA

A Grafton Paperback Original 1989

ISBN 0-586-20366-4

Printed and bound in Great Britain by
Collins, Glasgow

Set in Times

In loving memory of Poppy,
and for Pascal

PROLOGUE

Moscow: February 1984

The Boeing was practically empty: a couple of Northern students off to take an intensive course in Russian at the Pushkin Institute, a party of steelmen busy piling up empty beer cans before them, a retired couple on a second honeymoon in the wrong season and, further away in the first-class compartment, three professionals – businessmen, journalists, diplomats or all three – uniformly grey-suited, uniformly silent, on a routine trip to Moscow.

And then there was Masha, now known as Mrs May Harris. She kept bobbing up and down the aisle like an inquisitive squirrel in a vain attempt to while away the time by fraternizing with passengers and crew. 'My grandfather was a railwayman from Nottingham,' she began, as she always did, setting out her credentials for scrutiny. 'My grandmother was a nurse. They went to Russia after the revolution and spent the rest of their lives trying to get out. My mother and I finally managed it in 1954 after Stalin's death. And now, I am going back for the first time. To visit my sister. They wouldn't let me in before now . . .' A whispered exchange and then Masha's voice again. 'No . . . He is not my husband. My husband died some years ago and we were divorced long before that. This is my MP who is very kindly acting as my escort.' Hugo nodded and smiled. That too was part of the ritual. Masha resumed her tale. 'When my grandmother first arrived in Moscow they put her in a hospital where she had to look after these children who'd arrived from the Ukraine. Orphans of the revolution. They were filthy.

9

When she bathed them, the top of the water was solid scum. Lice. The children were covered in lice.' A silence fell and then, clear as a bell, he heard her voice as if she were speaking direct to him, and perhaps she was. 'Even after all these years, I'm scared. I cannot help feeling that they'll chuck me into clink the moment I land in Moscow.' She and her mother had left Russia on a tourist visa and it was only five years later that they were naturalized – anything else was far too complicated. 'I feel this nervous tension when I think of the way it was. The constant surveillance. Informers. The KGB. The terror of the secret police. That kind of experience leaves you scarred for life.' But now something stronger than fear was drawing her back to old mother Russia.

Silently, she resumed her place by his side, and sat, unusually still, staring out at the endless expanse that was Russia. The land, under occasional drifts of snow, was locked in the grip of winter. 'All that oppression and yet warmth too. Friendliness. People would come up to you, put their arms around you and say, "How are you, my old friend?" No one did that to me in England.' Masha's voice had become more heavily accented. He patted her hand comfortingly. She was a slight, lonely woman in her late fifties. 'I used to think it was because I was a foreigner. But we are all foreigners on this earth, aren't we?' The stewardess announced that they were due to land, and soon the runways of Moscow Airport emerged below them, clear black lines in the surrounding snow. The plane landed and was towed away to one side with other Western aircraft. Aeroplanes from Eastern Europe were parked elsewhere. East, West, the divide started here. On the tarmac outside, two militiamen in fur hats, grey overcoats and long boots took up position on either side of the plane, guns slung across their chests.

Masha stumbled as she stepped on Russian soil. She clung to Hugo, her fear palpable. In her princess-style black coat with its fur collar and hem she seemed like a throwback from the Fifties. He looked at her. Under the ash-blonde hair, the features were unmistakably Slav – the broad face, the high cheekbones, the narrow eyes. It had never occurred to him to ask her the nationality of her father, and now there was no need to ask. Her father, of course, was Russian.

'This airport is a depressing place,' he said casually, trying to make light of his own unease. 'Did you know it was built by the Germans in the late Seventies for the Moscow Olympics? Very German in style, isn't it? Reminds one of Hanover Airport minus the duty-free shops, doesn't it?' Shoulders hunched, head bent, Masha was pressing forth, staring blindly ahead, heedless of her surroundings in the arrivals lounge, until her gaze fell on the man at the passport control desk and she stopped dead in her tracks, too exhausted and too scared to venture further. The other passengers on their flight moved ahead and left. Hugo took Masha's arm and moved forward, moving her forward with him. His passport was cleared. And then it was Masha's turn.

The controller examined her travel documents, a letter in Russian, her passport. He took notes, asked questions, logged in the monosyllabic replies she delivered in a dead voice and let her through. They were through and they were on their own – the passengers on their flight had all gone. Hugo picked their cases off a carousel and they walked into a customs hall that seemed suddenly packed full of people. They joined a long queue where no one spoke either English or Russian and were still queuing there an hour later. He went up to a militiaman who could not understand what he said and then, looking

11

back, he caught sight of Masha still standing in the queue, silently weeping.

'Don't cry,' he said. The militiaman came back to them with an interpreter who told them they were in the wrong place, the queue for Eastern Europeans. It seemed curious to him that they should be subject to a more rigorous control than travellers from the West but when at last they had cleared customs – very much more swiftly this time – they found Masha's assembled relatives waiting for them and Masha was suddenly engulfed in great waves of Russian emotion and warmth.

They all left after he had promised to visit them before returning to London, and as Masha turned towards him a last time with a little wave that was intended to be appealing but which suddenly seemed grotesque, he thought wearily, poor cow. Little does she know that she is the decoy they used to get me here.

The woman at the Intourist booth told him that his contact had assumed he'd missed the flight from London and had returned to Moscow. Hugo laughed. The woman comrade was vaguely offended by his merriment and decided to ignore him. He was still laughing as he walked out of Scheremetjewo Airport.

Security men the world over wear the same split mask, he thought. Machiavelli on one side, bungling incompetent on the other. The closer you get, the less easy it is to see that cock-up is only the other face of conspiracy.

His laughter died on his lips when he stepped out. The cold was like no cold he had ever experienced before. It brought tears to his eyes that froze on his face. He felt overwhelmed, obliterated, utterly alone.

All around on the drive to Moscow were flat, snow-covered fields with the occasional ploughs clearing the snow off the motorway. 'Is this your first time in

Moscow?' asked the taxi driver. He was a stocky man with pale-blue eyes and grey hair. 'There is something I want to show you.'

They stopped briefly at a special area at the gates of Moscow.

'This is the closest the Germans got to Moscow during the war. There was nowhere to retreat. Behind us was Moscow. The Germans were in front. And so we fought. We all got together and fought. And we pushed them back. It was a turning point. And although we won, twenty million people died . . . I wanted you to see this so you can understand us.'

Hugo nodded. He remembered an old man, a constituent of his who had travelled all round Europe and Africa as a soldier during the war. He'd ended up in Germany after peace was declared. And what shocked him most of all was to find that the Germans – the beast, the enemy – were just like the folk back home.

The receptionist at the National was a brisk woman. 'Your voucher, your passport and your credit card, please,' she asked, hand outstretched. 'And now, please fill in this form and the porter will show you to your room.'

They stepped into an old lift cage of polished oak, which rose jerkily and ground its way to the third floor where the porter pulled open the heavy iron grille doors and let him out. An old woman in black was sitting at a small table and she got up and led him down a high-ceilinged corridor where a new red carpet failed somehow to relieve the overall impression of faded grandeur. They stopped outside a pair of tall, narrow wooden doors which she opened with a long key and he stepped into a room that was all at once vast, ornate and shabby. There was a sofa and armchair in each corner, but the bed was not in evidence. It was tucked away in a tiny lobby. The old woman closed the door behind her and he could hear her shuffling down the corridor. He went to the window. He could just make out the walls of the Kremlin in the surrounding dark.

Ivan Ivanov phoned the next day and they arranged to meet that evening at a restaurant in Gorky Street.

Ivanov was a large, surprisingly agile man in his early fifties who spoke fluent English with a heavy American accent. As they made their way into the restaurant a small crowd of porters and attendants came to help them out of their coats.

'You obviously have no unemployment problem here,' said Hugo with a straight face.

'No,' replied Ivanov, equally deadpan. 'Our unions are even more powerful than yours.' Quick responses and wit. A man to be reckoned with.

Hugo ordered a Georgian speciality, chicken *satsivi*, from an enviably long menu and whilst they waited for their order to come through, he and Ivanov broke bread. The warm peasant bread eaten with *sulguni*, the Georgian goat's cheese, was a potent appetizer but when, after a while, the waiter came back, he said that *satsivi* was no longer available. Hugo ordered chicken *tabaka* instead. But that too wasn't available. And then the penny dropped. On the tables all around them was the same dish of skewered lamb. *Shashlyk*. It was the only dish available that day. 'I'll try that,' he said.

'And what are your impressions of Moscow?' asked Ivanov.

Moscow 1984. The faded grandeur of ancient hotels. Food shortages. Black market deals with tourists for jeans, cameras or hard currency. Patriotic wall paintings

14

in the streets. Endless queues that tell you where the shops are. Chandeliers and polished marble in the Metro. And then, and only then, in the Kremlin churches, echoes of Holy Russia.

'Very cold in February.'

'You must have wondered why we brought you here . . .' said Ivanov, smiling good-humouredly. 'We have a job for you. The notebook. We want you to get it for us . . .'

'The notebook?' This wasn't what he'd expected. He brushed off the subject dismissively. 'It's nothing but the emotional outpourings of a neurotic woman . . . that kind of rubbish is of no earthly use to you or anyone else.'

'It's what lies behind the outpourings that we're interested in,' said Ivanov calmly.

'The secret messages in code?' Hugo scoffed. 'Fairy tales. Too far-fetched to be true.'

'Maybe, and maybe not,' said Ivanov. 'We won't know until we see the notebook.'

'And so the rumours are true, are they?' asked Hugo involuntarily. Uneasily, he looked over his shoulder. Ivanov laughed. 'You need not fear. There aren't many Englishmen in Moscow at this time of year. And besides, as you can see, this is a discreet spot.'

Hugo smiled. 'So this is the table reserved for KGB assignations, is it? Pity. I was rather curious to see your Dzerzhinsky Square offices at the Lubianka.'

Ivanov was not deceived by Hugo's subterfuge. 'Yes, of course, I'm with the GRU – the military wing of Soviet intelligence and counter-intelligence.' He smiled. 'You could say that I'm here on official duty . . . That is what you wanted to find out, isn't it?'

Hugo turned away. Someone had once told him, proudly, that his was a dirty job and that he was doing it

15

well, someone normally given to using expressions like integrity, duty and probity, but he could not now remember who it was. No matter, he thought. This business with the GRU was perhaps no different from any other negotiation. They wanted something out of him, but he wasn't prepared to deliver. 'It's more than likely that the notebook has already been destroyed,' he said. 'And if so, sending me on a wild goose chase can only arouse suspicion.'

'Our information is that the notebook has been hidden in a safe place,' retorted Ivanov. 'We want you to find it and hand it over to us.' There was something like contempt in his voice. 'I'll give you instructions on how to deliver it to our people in London.'

Hugo nodded. Humiliation was a kind of negotiating tactic. A way of intimidating the opponent and forcing your will on him. He pushed his plate away and rested his elbows on the table. 'You can drag this horse to the Volga,' he said in the quiet tones of a reasonable man, 'but you can't make him drink.'

Delicately, Ivanov sipped his Georgian wine. He held it up, looking at the bright liquid in the glass. 'Of course,' he said pensively after a while, 'we can't force you to do what you don't want to do. But even that implies a choice.' He smiled, like a man who knows he holds the winning hand. 'Accidents do happen in this turbulent world, don't they?'

Accidents. Sanctions. Dirty tricks. Hotel rooms creeping with bugs. The cock-and-bull accoutrements of cold-war skulduggery.

Around them people chatted and ate and drank. Hugo said nothing, waiting for the other man to continue.

'Accidents can so easily happen to a neurotic woman,

can't they?' he repeated in the same reflective tone, swilling the wine in his glass.

Angela, thought Hugo. Why should the GRU be so sentimental as to imagine he'd care a hill of beans what happened to Angela?

'We may have no option but to remove the little lady.'

Remove. Not kill, murder, assassinate or poison. Remove.

'You mean you want to kill Mrs Maitland Ellis?' He was struck by the surreal absurdity of the situation.

'Come now, we are no choir boys you and I,' said Ivanov reprovingly. 'Let us just say that it lies with you to make sure that she comes to no harm.'

And then he understood: they thought him enough of a soft touch to pay the price of Angela's life and work for them.

But the GRU were taking a gamble. One that might not come off.

'What do you want me to do?'

'Start by checking whether her home is bugged,' said Ivanov.

'And keep clear if it is . . .'

'On the contrary. Keep clear if it isn't. The notebook is no good to us if the little lady is in league with your security services.'

'And then?'

'And then, you must somehow get her to hand over the notebook to you.'

'Sexual entrapment? You must be very hard up to use me for a seduction job.'

'I am sure we have no lessons to teach you in that department,' said Ivanov coldly.

Hugo shrugged. 'It'll take a while . . .' Could he play for time?

17

'We are reasonable men,' said Ivanov. 'This is not a happy position for us, but we can live with our frustrations a little longer. Until Easter, say.' He looked Hugo straight in the eye. When he was not smiling, as he normally was, the heavy-jowled face seemed menacing. 'Easter is our deadline,' he said. 'Deadline,' he repeated, savouring the word. 'Deadline,' he said again.

'Though *stay of execution* might perhaps be more appropriate, in this case?'

Ivanov smiled indulgently. 'You English have such a strange sense of humour.'

PART ONE
Through the Looking Glass

1

The woman was plain. Under the long, grey hair, straight
as a girl's, the face was hard, the mouth pulled down, the
eyes lined.

That's me, thought Angela. She smiled politely at her
reflection in the glass and reached down to her bag for a
lipstick. Her fingers touched the edge of an envelope. She
pulled it out and opened it. Inside was a single black and
white photograph, blurred and grainy. It showed a tall,
slender girl in a white tunic standing at a bar with a man
in evening dress. All around them were boys and girls in
duffel coats and college scarves.

'Was that you then?' Lisa, the hairdresser, was peering
at the picture over Angela's shoulder.

'You'd hardly recognize me now, would you?' Angela
said, almost apologetically. I was beautiful then, she
thought with some surprise. Why hadn't I known it?

'But it was a long time ago,' she added, looking from
the girl in the photograph to Lisa. 'I was twenty. Your
age, perhaps?'

And what lies between Lisa and me is only time. Elvis.
The Beatles. Vietnam. Czechoslovakia. Afghanistan. Nic-
aragua. The Peace Movement. The Women's Movement.
The moon – one small step for man, a giant leap for
mankind. Teds, Mods, Rockers, Hell's Angels, Hippies.
Neo-punks like Lisa with her pink and yellow hair standing up in gelled spikes.

'A bit peculiar, isn't it?' said Lisa, reaching out for the
photograph.

This is the age of the common man, thought Angela, looking at Lisa, liking her. Hairdressers weren't like that in my day.

'Well, I mean to say,' added Lisa petulantly, 'there's you in fancy dress and then this bloke in his penguin suit and those scruffs all around paying not a blind bit of notice. What was this place anyhow?'

'The bar in the students' union at London University. ULU.' It wouldn't have changed that much in twenty years, would it? she asked herself.

'I was in a play, doing the part of a girl called Antigone. And the man was a guest speaker at some debate. I went to the bar during a break in dress rehearsals and we met. Someone took a picture for the student newspaper. That's all.'

Funny how a photograph could bring it back, that feeling of being twenty, of pushing forward to try out all those brave adventurous things that scared and thrilled you, playing the game, knowing it was only a game, a sham.

'Bet you fancied him,' said Lisa. 'Reckon I'd fancy him myself.'

She'd gone up to him at the bar and said something silly like, 'Haven't I seen you somewhere before?' And that too was part of the game. He'd laughed. 'No, that's not it, not it at all. I have seen *you* somewhere before, that's how it should be, surely?' And there and then, for no reason at all, the world stood still, stars exploded, the lightning struck and the miracle happened – connected-ness. A fake miracle. *Coup de foudre* schmaltz.

'Did you marry him?' asked Lisa, handing back the picture.

'No,' she said and put the photograph away. 'I married his stepbrother.' David. My husband, David Maitland

22

Ellis, no more mine than clouds floating in the sky. 'It was he who came across this clipping the other day and suggested that I should turn it into a photograph.'

Lisa nodded, losing interest. She ran her hands through Angela's hair. 'Dry, it's so dry,' she said, boredom blurring her words. Another head, another chore. 'What shall we do with it, do you think?'

'What shall we do with it?' echoed Angela. The wasted years. The failed marriage. The empty nest. Did women have breakdowns sitting quietly like this waiting to have their hair done?

'We could touch up the grey, if you like,' said Lisa.

Outside, the winter sky was pewter. The salon was decorated like a tropical forest with plastic fronds hanging down from fake rafters. Girls chattered and twittered all around them.

'Change me,' she said ruthlessly, staring her reflection in the eye, not bothering to look at the yellow and pink spikes on top of Lisa's head.

And then it was too late to change her mind. They washed and cut and coloured her hair and sat her down under a diffuser to dry it.

'Wait for me, don't go,' he'd said and she'd hung around self-consciously, waiting for the end of the debate, almost hoping that he would be disappointed to see her as she was in her black slacks, polo neck sweater and duffel coat, almost hoping that they would shake hands and say goodbye. She was a small-town girl who'd kicked over the traces of her suburban upbringing to find what she thought was a kind of freedom in the scruffy, unconventional bohemianism of student life in London in the early Sixties. And Hugo, who was then almost thirty and was beginning to feel himself middle-aged, saw her as a kind of curio, a

23

rebel and free spirit wholly unlike the confident, sophisti-
cated women who normally attracted him. He introduced
her to David, his stepbrother. They went out together
and sat through *Jules and Jim* twice, David and Hugo's
arms linked across her shoulders. They took her to parties
in the resident clerk's flat in the Foreign Office and she
took them to parties in derelict flats with murals painted
by students at the Slade. It was to David that she turned
when, more goose than swan, she discovered she was
expecting Hugo's child. They met in St James's Park one
lunchtime and she'd burst into tears as they watched a
flock of ducks on Duck Island. He handed her a handkerchief. Hugo was about to get married to someone else, he
said, and of course there wouldn't be much point in telling
him now. 'What are you going to do?' he asked.

'Have it, what else?' she said. She looked into his eyes
that were the colour of forget-me-nots and she knew then
what to do. 'Marry me,' she said. 'Marry me until it's
born.' It. Tom. And after Tom, as if by accident, the
twins, David's daughters. And the trap slammed shut on
him.

'Look,' said Lisa, 'isn't it nice? A kind of teddy-bear
colour.'

Angela saw a tall, wide-eyed woman with sloping
shoulders and a gleaming head of hair the colour of
orange marmalade.

She felt invigorated by the cold air as she stepped out into
Regent Street. A man turned to look at her. There was
life still in her, and beauty – curled, coloured, conditioned
– but still a kind of beauty. I am forty-one and I have a
self to recover, said a mocking voice inside her. And the

same voice said, fat chance. Fat chance. And besides, why do I do all this?

'Why do you do all this?' And this time the voice in her head was David's. David as a state of mind, a fear of falling short of standards he'd set.

And yet, and yet. The real ambition, he'd said to her once, the real ambition is to accept oneself as a slob and not care. A slob like me? she asked and he laughed. And you a school teacher, he said. You should know that the feminine for slob is slut. And yes, you could do with being a little more of a slut . . .

As she walked through the streets of Soho the school teacher in her tried to recall some lines of Baudelaire's about the sinuous folds of old cities where everything turned to enchantment. But what had Soho to do with Baudelaire or Baudelaire with Soho? 'You see only what you want to see,' David had said to her once. 'You see the world as you imagine it, as you think it should be.'

'And what's wrong with that?' she'd asked.

'It's a lie. Life's not like that. And besides, the dream is too thin.'

It was too thin for him. He had other dreams. Dreams she knew nothing about. And after twenty-one years of marriage, she felt she still did not understand him, for there was a side of him, the heart of him perhaps, that she did not know.

There was a time after the twins were born and before Hugo came to live with them after his first divorce, a time when she and David had been in love and discovered themselves anew. It was he, the conventional civil servant, who was the committed socialist and it was through living with him that she came to discover her own total lack of political conviction. Detached and objective where she was emotional and impulsive, confident where she was

25

insecure, precise where she was careless, it was nevertheless he and not she who was the passionate one. One by one, he unpeeled the layers of her personality as left-wing rebel and latter-day beatnik to reveal what he thought was her naïve and sentimental belief in the idea of romantic love.

'You only say that because you do not love me,' she'd say.

She walked past the boutiques, the restaurants, the wine bars. They were only themselves – restaurants, boutiques and wine bars. Look at things as they are, she told herself. Don't turn them into something else. She came to the top of Wardour Street where, in the window of a sex shop, a life-sized rubber doll sat astride a wooden chair. She had never managed to be enough of a slut for him. Perhaps it was the revenge she'd extracted on him for that part of his heart and mind that he kept closed to her.

But the failure of their love was academic now. They had not slept together for two years and it seemed that the marriage had died.

The cold January day was drawing to a close as she made her way towards Shaftesbury Avenue and stopped at St Anne's Churchyard. The derelict tower with its cube-shaped clockface stood proudly on the devastated site of St Anne's, destroyed during the Blitz. Some six or seven years before, she and David had strolled around the gravestones on their way to a theatre nearby to see a play about spies. He had pointed to the inscription on the grave of Theodore, King of Corsica – 'The grave great teacher to a level brings/ Heroes and beggars, galley-slaves and kings./ But Theodore this moral learn'd 'ere dead/ Fate poured its lessons on his living head/ Bestow'd a kingdom and denied him bread.'

'Nice,' she'd said.

'Nice,' he laughed, his voice shrill with derision.

'Nice,' he repeated with such venom that it brought tears to her eyes. 'I met a man who wanted to turn his life into a musical,' he said, as if attempting to show her what an appropriate response might be. And for all his socialism and her own lack of social commitment, that fastidious concern for doing and saying the right thing had seemed to her then like the most damaging form of intellectual snobbery.

As she stood at the foot of Theodore's grave a bedraggled woman dragging two plastic bags after her sidled up and held out an open hand. She wore a heavy coat under two layers of newspaper and seemed packaged like a parcel. 'Have you got the price of a cup of tea?' she asked. When Angela placed a pound coin in her hand she spat out an insult and scuttled away.

Angela shivered. She felt the bag lady's insult as a kind of curse and could not shake off a sense of foreboding, an obscure fear, not for herself but for David.

As she made her way to the gate, she spoke aloud the words on the gravestone. 'The grave great teacher to a level brings heroes and beggars.'

Where was David now?

2

The woman in blue overalls at the reception desk of the Department of Trade and Industry's offices in Victoria Street told her that there was no response from Mr Maitland Ellis's office, and would she care to come back after lunch. As Angela turned to leave she caught sight of a familiar face and she smiled at the man, recognizing him as someone she had met the month before at a Christmas party. The man signed her in and showed her to the office of David's secretary, Harriett Osborne. 'I suppose all this strikes you as very casual and informal after the MOD,' he said as he left her in Harriett's office.

'Yes, indeed,' she said. 'They wouldn't let me loose without an escort in permanent attendance at the MOD.'

David had spent most of his working life at the Ministry of Defence except for a spell on the secretariat at No. 10. His progress up the ladder had been meteoric and culminated with his promotion to Deputy Secretary at the age of forty-four, five years previously. He had seemed set for even higher things when, the year before, he had been suddenly and abruptly transferred to the Department of Trade and Industry. Earlier that year, in January 1983, their daughter Fanny had been charged with breach of the peace at Greenham Common. 'Well Pa, I've blown it for you,' she said. 'Thanks to me, there's a black mark on your record, and it's there to stay.'

'You know what they say about sowing the wind, don't you, Fanny?' he'd said calmly.

'That's Dep Sec speak, Pa; it's a mandarin cliché,'

retorted his daughter. 'And besides, I'm not scared of reaping the whirlwind.'

Harriett Osborne's office was empty. It was a modern room with large windows and grey, plastic-topped furniture, and there were two computers, one of which was used as a word processor. But there was nothing there to give any indication of the occupant's personality.

Angela remembered the office of Miss Smith, David's previous secretary, where carefully nursed plants lined the windowsills like toy soldiers.

Harriett's desk was clear of papers except for two blue HMSO diaries. The smaller one had weekly entries only. The other – David's – had individual day entries on each page.

Idly, Angela opened both diaries at the next day's page. David's diary was clear. In Harriett's diary the date was marked with a red circle and there was a brief entry: 08.40 NY.

This seemed odd to Angela. David wasn't due back until the following week, and he would be returning from Boston, not New York. She closed both diaries and moved through the inter-communicating door into David's office. Here too, there were no personal touches. His old office on the sixth floor of the Thirties-style MOD building was an imposing room with an Empire desk, eighteenth-century bookcases, ancient velvet curtains and the regulation white net safety curtains.

'Who are you and what are you doing here?'

Harriett Osborne was standing behind her and for a moment Angela thought she was about to strike her. And then, glancing uncertainly from her orange hair to her face, Harriett recognized her. Without further ado she turned on her heels and went back to her own office where Angela saw her check the two diaries before locking them away in a drawer.

'I am sorry to have startled you,' said Angela.

The woman took off her Burberry coat and red woollen scarf and regarded Angela coolly, as if nothing had happened. 'Have you been here long?'

Angela shook her head.

'Let me make you a cup of tea,' said Harriett. 'The urn is down the corridor. I won't be a moment.'

She was a slight, attractive woman in her late twenties with dark curly hair and small, sharp, brown eyes behind aviator-type glasses. She had won a first-class honours degree in PPE at Oxford and Angela knew from David that her special interest was moral philosophy.

'Force of habit,' she said when she came back. 'Well, you know what security was like at the MOD . . .' She handed Angela a cup of tea. 'What can I do for you?'

Shortly after Christmas, David had left on a trade mission to the US with his Minister and Angela did not know precisely when he was coming back. But as she looked at the calm, composed woman before her, she could not help wondering why she had reacted so violently a few minutes before. Was she having an affair with David?

'Do you know when David is due back?' she asked. 'I'd like to meet him at the airport.'

Harriett shook her head. 'No,' she said, 'but I'll find out and let you know . . . Is there anything else?'

The tenseness was still there, just below the surface.

'How does what you do fit in with moral philosophy?' It was not quite what Angela meant to say, but then what she meant to say wasn't simply why should someone with a First in PPE work as a civil service secretary. It was

30

something else, something unsayable, like – are you in love with my husband?

Harriett's small eyes widened in amazement. 'How dare you?' she asked indignantly.

The excessiveness of that reaction seemed to confirm Angela's suspicions and she was weighed down with sadness. She put the white china cup on Harriett's desk and stared down at her hands, incongruously remembering the bag lady's begging hands. 'I know,' she said. 'Morality doesn't come into it.' Why should David not spring the trap and find love with someone else?

'It doesn't,' said Harriett firmly. She seemed to be thinking aloud, pursuing some private obsession. 'There is a school of thought in moral philosophy that holds that we should not concern ourselves unduly about whether people in authority are nice or not, or whether or not we approve of their actions, so long as they do what they do to preserve civilized life – even if that means behaving badly in the process.'

She seemed a little pedantic now, a bluestocking. Angela could have hugged her. It was of no concern to her whether or not David had behaved badly. She cared only that David wasn't having an affair with this earnest woman. She got up to go. 'Don't bother,' she said. 'I'll see myself out.'

It was only when she reached Victoria Station that she began to feel again that obscure but familiar sense of menace. She made her way to a telephone booth and as she looked up the airport enquiries telephone number she noticed dispassionately that her hands were shaking. Breathlessly, head bent, she leaned against the side of the box, waiting for the trembling to stop.

When she got through to Heathrow they put her on to

31

Terminal 3 arrivals. They confirmed that a flight from New York was due in at 8.40 the next morning. She would be there to meet it – if only to prove to herself that David couldn't be on that flight.

3

The North Circular Road was free of traffic in the early morning and she arrived at Heathrow within an hour of leaving Highgate. What a wasted journey this will turn out to be, she thought as she parked her car and made her way to Terminal 3.

The New York flight was listed on the arrivals board and she joined a small group of people standing by the barrier – two or three couriers, and a woman waiting for some children coming back to boarding school after the Christmas break. Some distance further away, holding himself apart, was a tall, thin man in a grey, pinstripe suit who stared so intently at Angela that she thought she might know him and smiled to acknowledge him. He did not respond; but she was unnerved to find that he went on watching her, as if keeping her under surveillance.

Her attention was diverted by a little army of Asian cleaning ladies who drifted past them as the arrival of the flight was announced. And then the passengers started coming through customs, a small crocodile of sleepy children in school uniform pushing its way forward to the woman standing next to Angela. They all started speaking together, raising their voices to make themselves heard. Their luggage had been left behind in New York, they said, and they did not know what was to happen now.

She almost missed him. Tieless, his shirt open at the neck under a trenchcoat, David was the last person to come out. She saw him stride past the group of noisy children and recognized him as one would a long-lost relative or lover, familiar and yet different, unlike his usual self. He exuded a kind of feline strength and something in her thrilled at the sight of him – her husband. Her husband walked past and shook hands with the stranger in the pinstripe suit. They slapped each other on the shoulder like men who have fought wars together or are about to go to battle. Without glancing at her the stranger said something that caused David to stiffen – a free man resuming an old burden. The stranger spoke urgently and then left.

With studied casualness David turned round and met her eyes. She had a sense of *déjà vu* as if she'd lived the moment before, like the rehearsal of a play whose outcome is fixed from the start. Then was now. Something that had unfolded in the long years they'd known each other was about to close. It was the end of the journey. The world swam before her eyes and he dwindled into a blurred image. She turned away. It was over. She wanted to leave. But he came up to her and pulled her to him so roughly that she stumbled and had to lean against him for balance. He held her to him, her head against his, propping her in what seemed for all the world like the embrace of lovers. And still she tried to draw back until she recognized in his body, as familiar to her as her own, a fear as deep as hers. Briefly, they clung to each other.

He made as if to lead her away then stopped in his tracks. 'Good Lord,' he said. 'Your hair. Have you dipped it in paint?'

'It's the punk look. Don't you like it?'

'No. It's hideous,' he said and laughed.

She knew that something was amiss; but whatever he was up to was his business. What concerned her was their life together.

'What's happened to your glasses?' she asked as they

were walking out of the terminal building. He laughed and did not answer. 'You look different without them . . .'

'What do I look like?' he asked, amused.

'An adventurer,' she said. It sounded brutal. 'You look like you should be in films.' Make it light, she thought. 'One of those spy movies, perhaps.' But that, too, was wrong.

'You're loony, you know that?'

Loony was what Hugo had called her all those years ago. Hugo and David. David and Hugo who'd made her the butt of their jokes. She felt tired suddenly. 'I don't know how to talk to you any more. Perhaps I never did.'

'Angela,' he said. 'Angela.' How she yearned for tenderness. 'Let's go home.'

She drove him back in the grey Jaguar he'd bought the year before. Eyes closed, he was resting and she noticed with a pull at the heart that his hair was thinning and his face was lined. He, too, was growing old.

'Keep your eyes on the road when you drive,' he said sharply. But after a while he added gently, 'I can read you like an open book.'

There was a streak of cruelty in him which was combined with a strange gentleness so that she never could tell where she stood with him.

'Kids all right?' he asked. 'Though why I should go on referring to these great hulking brutes as kids I really don't know.'

'No problems.'

'None that we know of, more like. Come, that's not unfair, is it?' He looked at her pensively. 'I don't mean Tom. Tom was always good. But the twins now – double trouble from the word go, weren't they?'

Tom had fitted almost unobtrusively into the pattern of

35

their lives, a pattern that was to be turned upside down when the twins arrived.

'Do you remember what they were like?' he asked. 'Two fat babies with black curly hair and startlingly blue eyes as alike as two peas in a pod. Funny how they changed afterwards, isn't it?'

Fanny and Sally had grown up rivalling for attention, forever fighting each other when they were not struggling together against someone else, remaining essentially interdependent as if one complemented the other. Sometimes they would almost unconsciously exchange roles. And so it was that Fanny the tearaway turned into a brilliant scholar and was now reading engineering at Manchester, whilst Sally the good child became an academic drop-out.

'You'd never guess they were twins now, would you?' said their father. Their features, which had been so similar when they were little, had refined into beauty in Sally and hardened into plainness in Fanny. Sally was trying to break into modelling in Paris. 'I wonder sometimes whether they overshadowed Tom,' said David. Tom, the quiet elder boy who had become a quiet young man reading Italian at Oxford. It was now two years since they had left home. 'They're grown up now,' David said.

Angela never quite knew what being grown up meant, although she suspected that David had always been adult, even as a child.

'And that at least has turned out well, hasn't it, the kids, I mean?'

'You make it sound so final,' she said.

He put his arm round her shoulders. 'We're into injury time.'

Wasn't that why she had taken a year off work? To sort things out for a divorce.

36

'You never were much good at looking reality in the face, were you?' he asked, and then added lightly, casually, as if it didn't matter, so that she knew instinctively that it mattered very much, 'And by the way, how did you know when I was coming back?' And from where? he might have said.

She told him of her visit to the DTI and the entry she'd seen in Harriett's diary. She said nothing about the talk she and Harriett had had about morality. What was there to tell?

They were now in Highgate and she drove up West Hill, turned into Millfield Lane and straight on to Fitzroy Park. They were home. They sat together in the car, silently gazing at the house they'd shared for twenty-one years. He got out first, leaving her to park the car in the garage. When she joined him in the house he handed her a postcard from Sally in Paris without looking up and went on reading a letter he was holding in his right hand. She noticed that the letter was written on blue paper and that he was wearing gloves. The envelope slipped to the floor and as she bent to pick it up she saw that it was addressed to her. She stood up, as in slow motion, and handed him the envelope. Their eyes met. He was regarding her coolly, detachedly, like the man at the airport had watched her. 'From Harriett, is it?' she asked. Her throat felt dry.

He handed her the note and took off the gloves, which he folded carefully and placed in the pocket of his jacket. Harriett's letter said that David and his Minister were arriving back from Boston the following Tuesday and that Angela might care to wait for them in the VIP lounge at Heathrow.

'Don't let on, will you?' said David. 'If anyone – anyone

37

at all – asks, you haven't seen me, and all you know is what is in that letter. Is that clear?'

'You're truanting?' she asked, as lightly as she could.

'Angela,' he shouted. 'This is serious stuff. It's no game. Tell me that you understand what I'm telling you. Tell me.'

Something was splitting up, something was about to shatter and break. It was herself. Her self. She could no longer think or take in what he said to her. She held her hands together to stop them shaking, but it was no good. 'Stop it,' she wanted to say, but could not find her voice. 'Stop it!' she screamed and went on screaming until she saw the tears in his eyes and stopped. 'Don't worry,' she said. 'It's nothing. It'll pass. I'll be all right in a minute.'

He led her to the sofa.

'I am afraid,' she said abjectly. 'I don't know why but I'm scared.' She gazed at him through her tears. 'Help me.'

'What have I done to you?' he asked, and the tenderness in his voice overwhelmed her. He reached out for her hand and, raising it to his lips, kissed it, kissing each finger in turn, then the palm and the wrist, looking into her eyes all the while, like a child afraid of being scolded, like a child asking for forgiveness. 'I want you,' he said. 'I want you.'

4

Her feeling of happiness brimmed over. It seemed incongruous when, the following Tuesday, she met David and his Minister and the Minister's private secretary in the VIP lounge at Heathrow. David was bespectacled and grey-suited and correct, every inch the conventional civil servant. She heard that he had been taken ill in New York the previous week and had thereby missed much of the official tour. 'Still looks rather pasty, doesn't he?' said the Minister. 'Look after him, my dear, and on no account let him come back to the office before he's fully recovered.'

David spent the next two days in bed and she almost came to believe, or pretended to believe, in his illness. She nursed him but they were strangely awkward together and deliberately avoided talking about anything that might be troublesome. And so they said very little.

When she woke up on Thursday morning she found a message from him telling her he'd gone flying at Biggin Hill. She didn't think too much of it at first, for she knew that flying was his way of working off the stresses and pressures of his job; but she worried about the weather conditions, which were particularly appalling that January.

He had made his bed and his room seemed curiously set in place, a stage ready for a performance. There was a copy of *1984* on the bedside table, and as she opened it at the place set by a bookmark she saw that he had underscored the lines of the ditty – 'Under the spreading chestnut tree, I sold you and you sold me.'

She heard the telephone ring and went to answer it from an extension in the room next door which David used as an office. It was a journalist. She told him David wasn't in, and the man said, 'There is a report in *The Times* that your husband was named on American television last night as someone who had been under investigation by MI5 for a suspected serious breach of security. Would you care to comment?' She wondered at her own utter lack of surprise. Under the spreading chestnut tree, I sold you and you sold me. 'Are you still there?' said the man. She put down the phone without answering.

His desk was unlocked. One drawer was slightly ajar. Inside it, well in evidence, was a blue folder marked in David's clear hand with the words *Angela's Effusions*, in which she found a notebook she'd used as a kind of diary at odd times and which she thought she'd lost. She heard the door bell ring and went down the stairs, still holding the notebook. She hid it under the cushions of the settee in the lounge and went to open the door as the bell was rung again, more insistently this time.

The men on the doorstep were dressed in plain clothes but everything about them proclaimed them to be policemen. 'I am Detective Chief Superintendent Cross and this is Detective Chief Inspector Atkins from Special Branch,' said the man in front. She showed them in. They ignored her invitation to sit down and remained standing. The Chief Superintendent looked around him. A homely, comfortable room, she thought. 'It rather looks as though you were expecting us,' he said. He had an odd way of throwing his head back when he spoke, eyes half-closed, spitting out his words in a slow, hammered staccato.

She tried to make light of the remark. 'Is that a coded message, Mr Cross, or is it simply that you're not used to a tidy home?'

The blood rushed to his face and the flesh turned crimson. 'I don't like your insolence,' he said, with deliberate rudeness.

Angela wasn't accustomed to being addressed in this way. 'This is my home and I'll thank you to remember it,' she said coolly.

'I wouldn't try that if I were you,' said the Chief Superintendent. He sat down on the settee.

'Try what?' she asked, genuinely surprised.

'Intimidating me.'

This was getting out of hand. 'Hasn't it occurred to you that you might be misinterpreting me?' she asked.

'I've dealt with people all my life,' he replied unhesitatingly, 'and I have enough experience to understand your motives.'

And then she understood. He was trying to tell her that it was no good behaving like a mandarin's wife and that something had happened that had driven her beyond the pale. She nodded and waited for him to speak.

'Your husband is to be charged with offences under Section One of the Official Secrets Act,' he said, watching her reactions.

'Section One,' she repeated. 'Treachery, is it?' The word rung out like a sentence, confirming the divide between them. She was the enemy's woman, his accomplice perhaps, and he, the Chief Superintendent, was the upholder of law and order.

'He is suspected of having communicated information useful to an enemy,' he said bleakly, still watching her. 'I must ask you to tell us where we can find your husband.'

Was David trying to escape, then?

They were too late. When they phoned Biggin Hill they were told that he had already taken off for Dublin. She

41

heard them make arrangements for him to be arrested on arrival. And then they shut the door of the lounge and went on making a number of other phone calls from there.

The net was closing in, she thought. If only he could get away. Anywhere in the world. Out of their clutches. Safe.

He had betrayed her, she thought despairingly. From whatever motive, he had planned to expose her thoughts and fantasies to the scrutiny of strangers. He had betrayed her as she too had betrayed him, for she had never understood that he was on a knife's edge, leading a double life.

How irrelevant now, how lopsided, her views of love and happiness. The fact was that they had lived side by side without knowing each other. It had all been a terrible waste.

'I'd like to ask you a few questions,' said Mr Atkins. The Chief Inspector was a tall, gangly man who wore a constant smile on his face – Mr Nice to the Chief Superintendent's Mr Nasty.

'I'm ready to help you,' she said.

'Would you say that you have a good relationship with your husband?' he asked, almost jauntily.

'Yes,' she said automatically.

'And yet, you seem to lead separate lives?' He was still smiling.

'We live together.' Keep the target small, as David would say.

'You live together as man and wife?'

'We sleep in different rooms but have a normal sex life.'

'There is no strain in your relationship?'

'None.' She remembered his aphorisms, his Dep Sec Speak. Remember Talleyrand, he'd tell Fanny. *Speech is a capacity given to man to conceal his thoughts. Surtout pas trop de zèle.*

'Have you noticed anything unusual in his behaviour lately – that he was moody or withdrawn perhaps, or that he distanced himself from you?'

'No,' she said.

'And yet his colleagues were led to believe that his marriage was on the rocks.'

'They must have misunderstood him,' she said.

'Your replies are very pat,' said the Chief Inspector. 'Did you really have no doubts about him at all?'

She hesitated. 'I know that my husband is a good and honourable man,' she replied at last and heard Mr Atkins laugh good-humouredly.

'That's what they all say. Wives. The wives of villains. My husband is a good and honourable man. It is an archetypal reply. It means nothing. In nine cases out of ten a woman stands by her man. It's human nature I suppose. Or self-deception.'

She shook her head. If there was one thing she had never doubted it was that in his own way and by his own lights David was honourable, whatever that meant.

He waited and then went on, almost gently. 'Did you know that he has been under interrogation by MI5 over the last six months or so?' He had dark eyes that revealed nothing. A wall. 'If I may say so,' continued the Chief Inspector, 'you should be a little more concerned about your own skin or you may find that your head is also on the chopping block.'

He was still smiling.

And then the searchers, one of whom was a woman, arrived with warrants signed by the Chief Metropolitan

43

Magistrate. The search took seven hours. They began by taking up all the floor boards and went on to turn the place over. Every room, cupboard, drawer, book, file, photograph and letter was examined, recorded and then put back in place. A framed document hanging in the upstairs lavatory caused great excitement and was taken away for examination. It was a note from a past Prime Minister to a colleague in the Cabinet informing him that the Queen was to be asked to dissolve Parliament by proclamation so that a general election could be called. They found various official documents in David's desk, some of which were marked with security classifications which had been scored over in red, and these papers too were removed for examination. The drawer in which Angela had found the blue folder was empty; but when they tapped the bottom they found a secret compartment in which were a miniature camera, a roll of film and microfiche films. These too were taken away.

'Why don't you take this down to Deirdre?' One of the men handed her the copy of *1984*. 'It's Deirdre who's checking the books.' They wanted her out of the way and she did as they told her. It was as if they had taken over not only her home but also her self.

Downstairs in the lounge, Deirdre, the Detective Inspector, was standing before the bookshelves lining one wall, taking books down from the shelves, leafing through them and then putting them back in their place. A small pile of five or so books stood on the coffee table behind her: books she wanted to examine further, no doubt.

As she looked around her, Angela realized that the room itself had not yet been searched, and with a blow to the heart she remembered the notebook she had hidden under the cushions of the sofa. Unless she did something now, they would be sure to find it. But should she do anything at all? She could not shake off the feeling that what was happening now in this house had somehow been set up by David for reasons known only to himself, and that the notebook was part of that scenario. Was he trying to protect her by showing that she was too much of an idiot to be in any way implicated in treachery? But no, she thought, no. There was nothing but contempt in the word he had used to describe the notebook – effusions, her effusions, Angela's effusions. Whether or not he had intended it, the result would be to expose her to ridicule. It was a gamble she could not afford to take – she had too little dignity left to risk being left with none.

She walked up to Deirdre. Deirdre, still holding an open book in her hands, looked up. She was shorter than Angela. She stepped back.

'I am afraid your mates up there don't want me in their way and they've palmed me off on to you,' Angela said as she thrust David's copy of *1984* at the other woman. Deirdre struggled to catch it and failed, and one and then the other book slipped out of her hands to the floor. 'Your mates want you to examine this rubbish because they claim that's your business . . .'

Deirdre said nothing and turned her back to Angela.

Poor cow, thought Angela. She swept around the room picking up every written or printed piece she could find – letters, telephone directories, magazines, newspapers – and also the notebook, which she retrieved from the sofa and pulled out of the blue folder.

Deirdre had seen nothing of all this. She was poring over *1984*, examining each of the sidelined passages. 'Strange the things he marked,' she said. 'Like this bit with Julia and Winston. They are prepared for anything – losing their identities, living as waiters, committing suicide

45

– everything, but this. They will not agree to separate and never see each other again.'

Silly cow, thought Angela, her nerves jangling. Silly, compassionate cow. Hysterically she threw the magazines, newspapers, letters and directories at Deirdre. 'Do you want to see this and this, and that? Look. It's a notebook. A kind of diary. A personal thing. Mine.'

The woman ignored everything but the notebook and Angela was beginning to think she'd made a mistake.

As she leafed through the notebook entries Deirdre paused once or twice to look at Angela. 'Yes,' she said. 'I know what you mean. Men sometimes gang up on women and they cut us out, they freeze us . . .'

Angela didn't know and didn't care what she meant.

The policewoman hesitated, seemingly in two minds about what to do. And then she tore two pages out roughly from the notebook and handed the rest back to Angela. 'We'll examine these in detail to see if there are any hidden messages or whatever, and will return them to you later . . .'

It could so easily have gone the other way. She could have taken the whole of the notebook, adding it to her little pile of documents to be looked at in more detail.

And then someone came to tell Deirdre that she was wanted outside, and she left. Angela was alone. She stood in the middle of the room and picked up the copy of *1984*, looking for some kind of message in the sidelined passages. She came upon a sentence that said, 'All you care about is yourself.'

It was only when they had finished the search that the Chief Superintendent told her that David had not reached Dublin. His aircraft was missing and radio contact with him had been lost after he had stopped for refuelling in

Cardiff. An RAF helicopter crew had spotted the wreckage of a plane on the Reseli Mountains near Fishguard but it was now dark and the weather conditions were very bad in the mountains. There was apparently nothing more that could be done until the following day.

The ground had opened up from under Angela's feet. She felt she was falling. A hand reached out to steady her. It was the Chief Superintendent.

'Is there anything I can do for you?'

She shook her head. As if from far away, she saw him leave the room, heard his footsteps, the sound of voices, the slamming of doors, cars driving away. Her world had become unhinged but all was quiet and peaceful around her and it seemed almost as if nothing had happened, were it not for the blue folder she held pressed to her breast like a dead baby.

5

They phoned the next morning to tell her that a mountain rescue team from RAF St Athan in South Glamorgan had recovered a body at dawn. A car would collect her shortly and take her to the mortuary so that she could identify the body.

She remembered nothing of that journey except for a feeling of intense cold and numbness as if all winter had entered her soul. The mortuary was a nondescript building. Her arrival was registered and she was led into a room like an operating theatre in the centre of which was a table covered by a white sheet. Two men stood by. She turned to look at them, then someone swiftly removed the sheet and she stared numbly at the mangled remains of flesh and bone on the table. The flesh was charred to black carbon and the body was skinless. The skull was crushed, the head a Hallowe'en mask. A ring on the small finger of the left hand had begun to melt but the tiny diamond stone set in it remained intact like a tear. It was David's signet ring. She reached out and cradled the mangled hand in both of hers and kissed it as he, only a few days before, had kissed her own hand. He was nowhere in this room. His life was a spent candle. In the moment of his death she, miles away, had been unconscious of his agony. Gently, she laid down the withered hand and turned away. Yes, she said in answer to a question, yes it was her husband's body. She recognized his ring.

And as she looked through the tears at the man who'd asked the question, she thought she saw a light of triumph in his eyes and it was as if he'd slapped her.

6

Saturday. It was not yet dawn when Fanny set out on her
Kawasaki for the journey home. It was dark, the cold was
bitter, and she felt numb with grief, if grief was that
vacant feeling, that absence of feeling, that feeling of
absence from one's self. Nothing made sense any more. If
her father's life could be cut short stupidly by a piece of
machinery breaking down on a plane, then the whole of
life was like that too – meaningless. She couldn't come to
terms with her father's death, just as she couldn't cope
with the thought that he was a spy.

*'You know what happens when you sow the wind, don't
you, Fanny?'* 'Pa,' she shouted aloud to the air, the sky,
the wind, the nothingness around. 'It was you who reaped
the whirlwind.'

Authority had never frightened Fanny, because authority was her father and she the wayward, rebel daughter
who had always struggled against it. At ten, she had set
fire to some papers at school and was nearly assessed as
maladjusted until David appealed against the decision and
won. At eighteen, Fanny left home for Greenham
Common. She stayed there that winter, undeterred by the
cold, the boredom, and what her father called the sheer
dottiness of the venture. At Christmas she linked hands
with other women and they encircled the base, decorating
the fence with poems, with songs, with photographs, with
woollen webs, paper snakes and painted doves. A few of
them climbed over the fence and mounted their peace
protest on top of the silos. Fanny subsequently served

fourteen days in Holloway when she refused to be bound over to hold the peace. David could no longer help her then.

'Why do you do all this, what's the point?' he'd ask with pained incomprehension.

'You mean am I a loony leftie, a vegetarian lesbian?' she'd say, and it seemed very much like taunting except that he wasn't to know how near to tears she was. But there was no way she could get across to him. It didn't make sense to have nuclear weapons on spaceship earth if their only purpose was to destroy the planet, she'd say. But couldn't she see that there were other ways of thinking? No, she couldn't. Unlike her father, she wasn't into the business of papering over social cracks with woolly liberalism. She, Fanny, was in the business of changing things. In the end they compromised. Provided she took up her place at Manchester to do engineering the following session, he didn't mind what she did. 'But do this one thing for me, Fanny. Get yourself a decent degree.'

And now he had turned the tables on her, for if he had lived a life so separate and so different from that of the cool, rational, professionally fair administrator, it could only mean that there was a side of him that was the opposite of the one she knew, and she had never suspected it. But now that he was dead, the man behind the mask of authority had become utterly vulnerable, a victim, his life no more than a series of snapshots. The orphaned boy brought up by Alice. The registry office wedding to a pregnant girl. The children who arrived all at once and left home all at once, opting out as if it were an escape.

I've been a bad daughter, she thought. I've made him unhappy. Tears filled her eyes, blurring her vision. She stopped at a service station in the early hours of the morning and bought copies of all the daily papers. As she sat in the cafeteria, a steaming mug of coffee before her, she gazed at the newspaper photographs of her father, splashed out like convict mugshots before her, and she broke down into tears. Holding her head in her hands she sobbed loudly and uncontrollably like a child. Two youths at a nearby table laughed. 'What's up, boyfriend trouble?' She looked at them uncomprehendingly. Everything seemed the same as before, but a crack had opened up in the surface of the world, and nothing was the same any more.

She pieced together from the newspaper stories the series of events that had led to her father's death. The year before, a KGB defector had taken advantage of a field trip to seek asylum first in Western Europe and then in the USA, and it was this man who had provided the CIA with a list of Soviet spies in the West which included an agent codenamed Fitz who operated from the Ministry of Defence in London. When the list led to the successful unmasking of a Soviet agent in Berlin, the CIA pressed MI5 to investigate the case of Fitz, whom they had identified as David Maitland Ellis. But although MI5 interrogated David over a period of six months there was no conclusive evidence against him. It was then that the CIA tried to force the hand of MI5 by leaking information to CBS, knowing that once he had been publicly identified it was a foregone conclusion that charges would be brought against Fitz. But David's plane crashed into the Reseli Mountains in Wales before he could be arrested.

Fanny fixed her helmet and climbed onto the motor-bike. Was he trying to escape then, was he tipped off, or did he kill himself? She wanted to find out, she wanted to

51

understand, if only to make amends for having so misunderstood him in the past.

When she reached home, the entrance to Fitzroy Park was blocked with traffic which overflowed into Millfield Lane as far back as the Russian Trade Delegation. A throng like a demented bank holiday crowd had taken over the private road by Hampstead Heath and was laying siege to their house. Camera crews were camped in their front garden and photographers were focusing their lenses on the windows, taking random shots here and there, as if waiting for something to happen. They looked at her curiously as she parked her motorbike at the side of the house, then surged forth when she reached the entrance and ran to let herself in, slamming the door behind her. The house was dark and seemed empty.

'Fanny, is that you?'

It was her mother's voice. Angela was in the bathroom, having her hair coloured by Sally. Talk of playing the fiddle whilst Rome burns, Fanny thought to herself, horrified at the incongruity of the act. Had they gone mad? As Angela turned from the handbasin brown dye streaked her face like tears.

'What's happening?' asked Fanny. The scene seemed surreal.

'Fan, stop asking silly questions,' said Sally, her voice shaking. She brushed a long strand of hair away from her face and as always Fanny had a little shock at seeing in her twin sister her own image, perfected. The door and phone bells started ringing together. Someone was banging at the door. 'Can't you do something about this racket?'

Leaning over the handbasin, Angela said nothing. She seemed utterly defenceless, a drowning woman.

Downstairs, Fanny disconnected the door bell and took the telephone receiver off the hook. Messages were pushed in through the letter box offering hundreds, thousands of pounds for an interview, a story, photographs. Fanny sealed it with brown parcel tape. She drew the curtains all round the front and the back of the house. And then there was a kind of hush outside, and as she pressed her head against the door she thought she could hear the sound of a car being driven up the lane. The noise intensified and then Fanny heard a familiar voice rising above the din. It was her brother Tom. She pulled open the door and he stepped in. Surrounded by shouting journalists, Tom and Fanny half-pushed, half-pulled their Great-Aunt Alice into the house, pushing the door shut against the hammering outside.

Through the door they heard a woman's voice rising above the others, starting a cry which others took up: 'Out,' they cried, half in jest. 'Out, out, out of the molehill.'

Tom was leaning against the door, less to buttress it than to support himself. 'We've ratted on them. They see us as a nest of burrowing moles,' he said despairingly.

His nervousness disappointed Fanny. 'You're mixing your metaphors,' she said. He shrugged his shoulders dejectedly, his tall gangly frame pressed against the door as if unable to detach itself.

Fanny turned to Alice. 'Are you all right?' she asked, kissing her on the cheek. Alice was leaning forward, gasping for breath. 'Animals,' said Fanny angrily. 'Animals who think nothing of harassing a defenceless old lady.'

'Old?' Alice rounded on her. 'Old?' she repeated, still breathless. She was seventy-five, a small woman with wavy grey hair and fine blue eyes, who still retained some

53

of the energy and combativeness of her youth. 'Is it a crime to be old?' she demanded. 'And what's wrong with "woman", for heaven's sake? Why can't you say "an old woman"?'

There was a noise on the landing and they looked up to see Angela coming down the stairs, her hair black and stiff like a wig. 'Angela, have you asked for police protection?' asked Alice.

'The last thing I want is police protection,' replied Angela in a vacant singsong. 'And besides, they're bound to leave soon. Tomorrow's Sunday.'

They stood like shadows in the darkened hall, listening to the rumble outside, not knowing what to do next.

The press was still there the following day. A pile of papers was left on the mat and cameras clicked as Sally stepped out to fetch them.

They were sitting together around the large kitchen table at the back of the house, with the yellow blinds pulled down and the lights on, the papers spread out before them. The story – as they came to refer to it, almost mythically – the story was banner headlines in all the papers. 'Riddle of Top Civil Servant's Death.' 'MOD High-Up in Espionage Scandal.' 'Man Identified in CBS Programme Killed.' 'Mystery Death of Whitehall Man.' They all projected much the same image of David – cool, sharp, rational, something of a cold fish, a man with few friends, a skilled and somewhat calculating administrator who seemed the perfect civil servant. There were references to his background, his father's death during the Battle of Britain, his education at Eton and Cambridge, the house in Fitzroy Park – 'London's last country lane in exclusive Highgate' – the car he ran – a Jaguar – the family home in Berkshire and a villa in the South of

54

France. But there was nothing to explain that the villa wasn't theirs and that the house in Berkshire had been turned into a school. Instead, a question was implied without being stated in so many words: how could a civil servant afford to keep himself in that kind of style, other than by the use of tainted money?

There were differing accounts about the information he had passed over, although they all seemed to agree that it was information connected with the Falklands. There were two main theories. The first, and more popular, was that he might have passed sensitive defence secrets to the Russians during the Falklands War and that, if communicated to the Argentinians, that information could have contributed to the sinking of HMSs *Coventry* and *Sheffield*. The second variant was that the information passed to the enemy was in fact a secret assessment of the performance of Britain's military equipment during the Falklands War. One or two papers implied that whatever was passed to the Russians also concerned the Americans and was sufficiently important to them to cause the CIA to bounce MI5 into action.

David's family hadn't escaped the Press's attention either. There were stories about Alice's communism in the Thirties, pictures of Sally in a bikini, of Fanny at Greenham, of Alice and Tom being hustled into the house the day before. A modelling agency in Paris was reported to have said that they had cancelled their contract with Sally.

'Never mind, love,' said Tom. 'When one door closes, the other will be slammed in your face. And it's not just you. We'll all have to learn to take the rough with the rough.'

Angela looked at her son but did not speak. She wore a black dress that was too short and too tight and there were dark circles under her eyes – the skin actually looked black.

'What seems evident,' said Alice, 'is that they have no idea whatsoever about how David might have operated if – mind you, I say if – he was a spy, whether he was part of a spy ring, who controlled him or how he managed to pass the information over.'

'That wouldn't be too difficult, would it?' said Tom. 'He went for a regular daily jog on the Heath and would have had no problem making contact with someone from the Soviet Trade Delegation up the hill.'

'But there is no real evidence, no hard evidence against Pa – it's all circumstantial stuff,' said Fanny. She did not know why she said it. Like Tom, she did not doubt now that her father had been a spy. She turned to Angela. 'Did the fuzz find anything when they searched the place?' she asked.

Angela hesitated. 'Classified papers, microfiches, a miniature camera, that kind of thing,' she said.

'Well, there you are. What earthly good is any amount of papers, films or microfiches to any prosecutor if there is nothing to say that the information has been wrongly disclosed and if there is no chance of interrogating your chief suspect because he's dead? None of this is any good without some other kind of evidence too . . .'

'What kind of evidence?' asked Angela. She was pitifully pale and drawn. 'What kind of evidence?' she repeated bleakly.

'A list perhaps.' Angela's intensity frightened Fanny. 'Imagine that you were passing stuff to some comrade up the hill. Would you not want to keep a record of what you'd given him and when?'

'What kind of a record?' probed Angela. She seemed to be straining not to lose her grip.

'Heaven knows,' said her daughter. 'Something totally innocuous that no one would suspect, perhaps.'

'Really, Fan. Give over, will you?' Tom was angry. 'It seems more than likely that Pa was a spy and I see no need to deceive ourselves. Face up to it. What he did was wrong and there's no excuse for it. You do not take the Queen's shilling and sell State secrets to the enemy. That's all there is to it. We can only judge Pa by the standards he gave us. The standards he lived by. Or pretended to.'

Angela stood up and walked out of the room. She seemed a little deranged in her tight black dress, clutching a white plastic bag to herself like some kind of comfort blanket. What was in that bag? wondered Fanny. What was her mother hiding in that bag? But why was she so unkind? She felt a despairing anger at the misery and fear around her.

'They've painted him as some kind of weirdo,' said Sally, reading one of the papers. 'An emotionally deprived character with a chip on his shoulder . . . He wasn't like that.'

Fanny got up.

'Where are you off to?'

'Out,' she said. And before anyone could stop her she was out of the house, her crash helmet under her arm.

Her path was blocked by the crowd and as she pushed ahead, trying to forge a way through for herself, the helmet was knocked out of her hands and was passed like a bobbing balloon to the back of the crowd. Like a cornered animal, Fanny turned on the crowd, hitting out with clenched fists. 'Buggers,' she shouted amidst laughter, and as they drew back she saw the cameras pointed at her.

A door slammed. Angela was standing alone under the porch, her face marble-white against the black of her dress, quietly watching the scene before her. Her sudden appearance unnerved the crowd. They looked up uncertainly, as if half-expecting her to vanish back into the house. She was utterly still. 'Let my daughter go,' she said. There was no mistaking the note of command in her voice. Like a peace offering, the crash helmet was passed back to Fanny and the human tide surged towards Angela. Microphones were thrust before her, camera shutters whirred and clicked, lights flashed. She looked straight into the eye of the cameras and spoke out. 'You have hounded and harassed my family for two whole days and your behaviour is inexcusable,' she said in a passionless voice. Fanny felt she was seeing a stranger – a strangely powerful woman who knew precisely what to say and how to say it. 'This is private property and you have no right to be here,' went on Angela. 'I want you to leave.'

There was a stunned silence and then a woman's voice asked, 'What about allegations that your husband was a spy?'

'My husband was a good and honourable man and the loyal servant of his country,' Angela replied without the slightest hesitation. 'The allegations made against him are based on conjecture, and the Press should at least wait until the facts are known before indulging in muck-raking and witch-hunts.'

The Press did not leave, but they grew perceptibly quieter. Gradually the curtains were opened inside the house, the telephone receiver went back on its hook, the entrance bell was reconnected, and Angela heard that the inquest on David's death was to be opened that Friday and that she was expected to attend.

She was out of the lounge when the television news came on, and they called her. She stood by the door as if transfixed by her image on the screen. 'My husband was a good and honourable man,' said the woman with the chiselled face. 'He was the loyal servant of his country.'

'The wife of the man suspected of espionage denies he was a spy and denounces Press harassment,' said the announcer.

'Good performance, Angela,' said Alice coolly, a note of sarcasm in her voice. 'The image of the brave wife and mother standing up to harassment is bound to attract you some public sympathy.'

7

The enormity of the task involved in identifying the causes
of David's accident was revealed at the opening of the
inquest, which Angela attended with Fanny. They heard
that the light aircraft in which David had been flying had
crashed into the side of the 1,700 feet Reseli Mountains,
having failed to clear the ridge by only 150 feet, and that
it had exploded on impact, bursting into flames. David's
body had been engulfed in molten metal, which solidified
as it cooled, and had to be freed from the wreckage. The
body was so badly burned and disfigured that it could be
identified only by a dental plate, a ring, and a set of keys.
The Accidents Investigation Branch of the Department of
Transport had been called to the scene as soon as possible
but full investigations would be required to ascertain the
causes of the accident, and meanwhile the inquiry was
adjourned. The burial of the body would not be allowed
before the inquest was completed.

That evening, back at home, Fanny took two mugs of hot
cocoa to her mother's room. Angela was sitting at her
dressing table, staring vacantly at her reflection, her hand
resting on the white plastic bag which she had taken with
her to the inquest.

'Haven't you had enough for today, Fan? Isn't it time
for bed?'

'I wanted to talk to you for a bit.'

'What's the matter?'

I've lost all sense of certainty, Fanny wanted to say. I

thought I knew what was right and wrong, and now I don't any more. The things I valued – peace, justice, truth – all these things seem irrelevant now, empty slogans. 'I don't know what I believe in any more,' she said.

Angela turned round to face Fanny and she nodded and stared down at her hands, which she started rubbing together as if to warm them up.

'Why did you tell them that Pa was a good and honourable man?'

'Because I believed it. Don't you? He was a good father, wasn't he?'

'Yes.' He'd cared for them – his children – with a love that was almost maternal. He'd led their games when they were little, organized their holidays when they were growing up, took them walking and climbing and swimming and skiing, and later, much later, when they considered themselves quite grown up, he went on trying to organize their lives, much as he complained that they had become too large, too noisy, that they overweighed the house with their presence.

Angela seemed to have forgotten Fanny. She was wringing her hands, twisting them, the white plastic bag still in her lap.

'What's the matter?' said Fanny. 'And what are you hiding in that bag?'

Angela rounded on her. 'What do you mean, what's the matter? The matter with me, or the matter with you? Good God, look at yourself.' She dragged Fanny before the glass. 'Look,' she accused. And Fanny saw a stocky, clumsy girl in black trousers and a grey sweater. Ugly. Yes, she was ugly where Sally, her twin sister, was beautiful. Cinderella's ugly sister. And she felt a little like that crazy child arsonist all those years ago.

'You fought, Pa and you. In this room. You thought we didn't know but we did. I used to lie awake at night listening to the sound of your voices as you shouted at each other. I was terrified that you'd split up and shatter everything . . .'

Angela relented. 'Stop fussing about things, Fanny,' she said. 'Whether or not your father was a spy was his business. A matter between him and his conscience. It has nothing to do with you. Get on with your own life. Don't waste it. Be happy.'

'Don't you want to understand what motivated Pa?'

Angela shook her head.

'But what if you have been living a lie? And if you're not bothered, why did you tell them he wasn't a spy?'

'Trying to get out of trouble seemed reason enough at the time . . . And besides, I didn't say he wasn't a spy. I said there wasn't enough evidence to prove he was a spy. It's not at all the same thing.'

'How do you know?'

'I don't. I'm just guessing.' She looked very tired. 'It's late,' she said. 'Go to bed, Fanny.'

Angela wasn't in when Fanny came down for breakfast the next morning. Apparently she had taken Alice's car to be checked at a garage in Crouch End.

'I didn't know there was anything wrong with your Mini,' Fanny said to Alice.

'Neither did I. In fact there isn't. But your mother had a notion the car wasn't safe and she wanted to make sure that there was nothing wrong with it.' She looked at Fanny. 'She seemed a little obsessed about it. I suppose,' she said, thinking aloud, as if trying herself to understand, 'I suppose that, as in dreams, a car is a symbol for one's

62

life. One's self. Still – why should your mother be projecting her fears on my car rather than her own?'

'Clean bill of health,' said Angela to Alice when she came back. She seemed more relaxed, more her normal self, than at any time since David's death. 'But you ought to have it serviced properly before long. Did anything happen while I was away?'

'Hugo phoned,' said Alice. 'He wanted you to know that he is there if you need help at any time.' Angela said nothing. 'Really, Angela, isn't it time you forgot those stupid quarrels all those years ago? You need all the friends you've got now and you have no better friend than Hugo.'

'Hugo who?' asked Fanny.

'Hugo Gray,' said Alice. 'Your Uncle Hugo. The MP. Surely you remember him, don't you?'

She remembered laughter and disturbance long ago when she was a child.

Angela's lips were pursed and she was frowning. It was her '*pas-devant-les-enfants*' expression.

But I am not a child any more, thought Fanny, and I recognize deception when I come across it. And then she noticed that her mother was no longer carrying the white plastic bag.

8

Fanny called the Palace of Westminster from a public telephone at Highgate tube station and was put through to Hugo's secretary when she asked to speak to him. She was his niece, she explained to the woman, and it was very important that she should see him that afternoon. 'You wouldn't by any chance also like a place in the public gallery for Prime Minister's Questions?' The sarcasm was as inescapable as it was inexplicable but Fanny readily assented and it was agreed that she would meet Hugo in the Central Lobby after Questions.

The public image of Hugo Gray was that of maverick right-winger and eccentric, a Little Englander who, having filed into the 'No' lobby when Britain joined the Common Market, then turned passionately pro-European and anti-American. He was the prophet of doom who inveighed against trades unions ('to those with most clout it shall be given the largest slice of the cake'), left-wingers ('the fruitcake politics of nutters and scroungers'), the IRA ('heartless, mindless savages'), feminists ('if more mothers stayed at home there would be fewer yobs'), and peace women ('if the monstrous regiment wants to work for peace it need only start by thinking with its head instead of its mouth'). This right-winger was disquieting to the establishment, and not only because he was wet to the point of sogginess when it came to social issues. A twice-divorced womanizer who loved the good life, he was raffish, outspoken, a rule-breaker whom his constituents adored but who would never achieve high office.

The Palace of Westminster was covered in a light dusting of snow from which, surrounded by scaffolding, Big Ben emerged like a pagoda on a stage set. Fanny's motorcyclist's gear very nearly caused the security scanners to break down at St Stephen's Entrance, but Hugo's secretary was there to meet her and showed her to the public gallery. 'Listen,' she said. 'Let me forewarn you: there has been a slight misunderstanding and you may find that Hugo does not know who you are.'

The MPs on each side of the Commons seemed oddly unreal, like waxwork figures rowdily come to life, and Fanny watched from the gallery as the Prime Minister walked in from the side of the Speaker's Chair and sat down on the front bench. When she stood up, the first question addressed to her was about her engagements for the day, and a somewhat half-hearted exchange followed as if the House was waiting for something else. Just after three-thirty the Prime Minister said that with the permission of the Speaker she would make a statement to the House about the Maitland Ellis Case. The House listened to her in silence as she said that David George Maitland Ellis was to have been charged with offences under Section One of the Official Secrets Act, including obtaining and communicating to an enemy information prejudicial to the safety and interests of the State, when he was involved in a fatal accident. An inquest was opened and had been adjourned pending the outcome of investigations into the circumstances of the accident and enquiries by the security service. It was too early to know whether the full inquest would be held in camera or whether the Security Commission would be asked to investigate the case.

The Opposition Leader asked that the Prime Minister should admit that the whole affair had been bungled by the security service whose hands had been forced by a leak inspired by the CIA. The Prime Minister waited for the cries of 'Resign' from the opposition benches to subside and then, her voice rising above the clamour, said that she would not answer hypothetical questions. A member on her side of the House then asked whether the Government intended to take any steps in view of the allegations that the case had major implications for the defence strategy not only of the UK but also of NATO, and again she took the line that she could not answer hypothetical questions. There followed questions about possible spy rings and whether the Prime Minister anticipated that further prosecutions would be made as a result of the case. She said that it was not appropriate at that stage to add to the details she had already given, and whilst she could neither deny nor confirm allegations, the House could rest assured that they were all being carefully investigated.

In the Central Lobby, Fanny saw a tall man with grey hair advance towards her. He had a military bearing and was formally and expensively dressed in a striped, dark-blue suit and lavender shirt. He regarded Fanny quizzically, his eyes lingering over the leather trousers, the CND badges on her jacket, the plastic helmet under her arms. He seemed amused. 'My secretary tells me that you are Fanny Hill, but she is liable to get things wrong.'

Fanny could not summon up the energy to feel insulted at what she supposed was a humiliating misunderstanding. No man had ever treated her like that before and she felt both attracted and repelled.

'Ellis,' she said neutrally. 'I've dropped the Maitland. It was too much of a mouthful. I am Fanny Ellis.'

And for a moment his composure deserted him. But the eyes that regarded her yielded nothing and the face was like a mask. He was old, thought Fanny, an old man of fifty. 'The silly cow didn't tell me . . .' he said at last. There were the beginnings of laughter in his voice and as Fanny looked into his eyes, his round, brown eyes that were so like the eyes of her brother Tom, she thought she understood what it was that her mother had been anxious to hide, and she felt a tear slide down her cheek.

'Fanny, dear child, don't cry,' said Hugo.

9

Thursday 26 January 1984. Angela is sitting alone in the lounge, watching a fire burn in the grate. A car drives up the lane and instinctively she looks up, consciously telling herself that it can't be David, he's dead. His image surges sharp and clear in her mind, filling her with the sense of his presence. She sees him in her mind's eye, she can see him smile his lazy smile, she can feel what he's like. One day, she thinks, one day his image will no longer be imprinted on me and then I shall have lost him completely.

She picks up two sheets of paper from the coffee table and reads them one more time, as if trying to memorize them. These are pages she has torn off from the notebook. Her notebook. One by one Angela burns the sheets of paper and feels she is immolating part of her life. The day exhausts her. Colour hurts her eyes. Noise bruises her nerves. She feels impaired. She remembers what it was like to be whole, in the same way a cripple remembers the motions of a waltz. The words dance before her eyes.

13 January 1970

They seem perfectly happy together, David and Hugo. They discuss things, play with the kids, take the piss out of me and send me up. And every time, I rise to the bait. But Hugo is in a bad way. With Jessica, he has lost a way of life. He drinks too much and is beginning to go to seed – he is not yet 37. David is the calm centre at the heart of the storm. He alone can help when Hugo sinks into a mood of black depression.

26 February 1970

To those who give, it will be given back. You are each of you,
transmitters of life: you pour life into what you do. I don't. I am
an appendage. Your friendship excludes me. You are in a league
apart, he and you, and I am your fall girl.

28 February 1970

Today you are 36. I say to myself these things that I cannot say
to you. Who are you? I say to you in my head. You are not the
man I married, says some archetypal shrew, and that is not what
I mean. It is just that at each stage of knowing you, I perceived
you differently. And so, who are you? Is that you, the poor man
who tries his best to be ordinary, who plays with the kids, sticks
to the middle way, and is saddled with a wife he can't abide?
Who are you behind your mask? What is it you're covering up?
Why this conspiracy with Hugo? Can't you see, it isn't me you're
betraying when you plot with him, it's you, the image I have of
you.

3 March 1970

Sleepless nights. I lie by your side dog-tired and wide awake.
You sleep and do not stir. A door bangs in the night. A dog
barks at dawn. Dogged days, dirty-water days with the cleaning
and the washing and Hugo complaining of his 'grubby' sheets.
Days when I think it's time to call it a day and see things for
what they are. And then a night comes that is sweetened with
love and I know then who the enemy is. It is this child-woman.
It is me.

29 March 1970

Easter Day. Happiness is being with you and the kids and no
one else. My kingdom. Whole like a good egg.

9 April 1970

Hugo is back. He is rehearsing a speech: 'Man is the only animal
that fouls its own nest.' And you, my love, you look at me with
a dislike so intense it looks like loathing.

13 April 1970

To get to this point, I must have travelled through valleys of hero-worship. But when their idols tumble, bitches are furies. I looked up to you once.

21 April 1970

Full moon. Lunacies. I am bloody to you, and you are bloody back, and I am even more bloody, and you are absolutely bloody, and that is our business because we have earned the right to our bloody-mindedness. But after the bashing and the shouting and the fighting, I am alone where no one can reach me any more.

Angela takes a pen and a sheet of paper from the bureau in the room and writes a new note:

26 January 1984

I have loved you for something you were not and you have seen me as someone I wasn't. We have lived side by side without knowing each other. It was a kind of misunderstanding. One day I shall no longer remember your smile or the colour of your eyes and it will no longer hurt me to think that you didn't love me. Can I make good? Can I learn to see things as they are and not feel afraid?

She burns the day's newspapers too. An article about five Greenham women goes up in smoke: the women were received by the Soviet Embassy and were then evicted by the Metropolitan Police Diplomatic Squad when they started protesting at the detention of a Russian peace woman – 'We come to you from Greenham Common where as you know women have been protesting for a long time against the weapons aimed at you, the Soviet people . . . The attempt to silence Olga Mdevedkova is not incidental, it is central to the issue.' The words President Reagan would like to say to the people of the

70

Soviet Union also turn to flames: 'A nuclear war cannot be won and must never be fought. The only value in our two nations possessing nuclear weapons is to make sure they will never be used. But, then, would it not be better to do away with them entirely?'

She feels implicated in war and peace, East and West, and the security of the nation. And yet the thought is inconceivable, ridiculous. She suspects that the notebook may somehow have contained details of the information David had passed to the Russians. And that too is ridiculous. She feels she is thwarting a plan carefully laid by David when he left the papers like an exhibit in the drawer of his desk. She is standing in his way because she does not want to be made to look a fool in the eyes of the world. And yet, neither does she want to be the enemy of her country. She's done what she's done in good conscience, but doesn't know whether it was right or wrong. And even now she wonders whether it isn't all in her mind, whether she isn't a little mad.

10

Friday 27 January. The door bell rang. It was eight o'clock precisely. Angela hadn't slept all night and she felt raw. Bleary-eyed, she opened the door. The Chief Superintendent was standing on the doorstep with Detective Inspector Owen. She let them in.

There was a smell of stale smoke in the lounge. The ashtrays overflowed with cigarette ends, and a framed photograph of David stood in the middle of the coffee table, propped up by an empty bottle of Scotch.

'I'm sorry to have to bother you again,' said the Chief Superintendent, 'but I should be grateful if you could let me have your notebook.'

'I am afraid you're too late,' she told him. 'I destroyed it. Last night. I burned it . . .' She pointed to the grate where a single touch of white emerged from the ashes – a half-singed sheet of paper with yellow-brown burn marks. Delicately she picked it up with two fingers and handed it to the Chief Superintendent.

'Do you know what you've done?' he asked, his voice like steel. He handed her back the half-scorched sheet and as she looked at it, she began to see that the text was underscored by an almost imperceptible series of dots, which she guessed were part of some secret code.

She went to the coffee table and picked up the photograph of David. He was grinning lopsidedly so that one side of his face smiled whilst the other grimaced. 'Let us go through this business of living without too much fiction,' he'd say. And now she wondered whether that's all they were, fiction, those fine principles he'd lived by, or pretended to live by – duty, integrity, conscience, responsibility.

A ritual of sorts: a police arrest, starting with the white Rover driving away at speed in a scream of sirens and flashes of blue lights; the search for a magistrate (in the event a builder's merchant) who signed the warrant without looking at her; the arrival at the police station where her personal possessions and her passport were taken away and placed in a labelled plastic bag; the taking of fingerprints; all leading to an interrogation in a small room.

'This interview is being tape-recorded. My name is Bernard Andrew Cross. The other officer present is Detective Inspector Deirdre Patricia Owen. Your name is Angela Stephanie Maitland Ellis. Your date of birth is 3 June 1942. I must caution you that you do not have to say anything unless you wish to do so, but anything you say may be taken in evidence and used against you. Do you understand that?'

Another ritual, another time. 'I do.'

She was taken through the circumstances that led to the identification of the notebook. 'A search was carried out at your house in Fitzroy Park, Highgate N6, and one of the officers carrying out that search, Detective Inspector Owen, here present, was engaged in searching through various printed publications when you handed her a notebook. Is that right?'

She felt on safe ground and saw no reason to hold back. 'Yes,' she said, 'that's how it was.'

'What was inside the notebook?'

'Jottings. Things I jotted down over the years. I suppose it was a kind of diary.'

73

'Why did you draw it to Inspector Owen's attention?'

'I thought she might need to see it.'

'Are you sure?' He regarded her with undisguised hostility. 'Wasn't it a ploy to head off any suspicion from yourself and the notebook?'

'It wasn't like that,' she said, fear in the pit of her stomach. 'It wasn't like that,' she repeated feebly.

He leaned forward, his eyes bright with excitement. The trail was red-hot. 'Why did you destroy the notebook before the sample pages could be examined?'

'My husband's death made me see how vulnerable we all are. In life we're in death and all that . . .' she trailed off. This would carry no conviction at all. She had no option but to go on. 'If anything happened to me, I did not want my children to come across the notebook and be hurt by what they might see there.'

He could smell blood. 'Why should they be hurt by that?'

'Because of the differences between their father and me.' It did not seem satisfactory as an explanation.

'Or perhaps because you were their father's accomplice.'

That night, she was locked up in a cell and slept on a bench under the glare of a naked light bulb till she was shaken awake the next morning and the interrogation was resumed.

They started off with questions about David. It was known that he went jogging in the mornings in the vicinity of the Soviet Delegation's offices in Millfield Lane. Had she known him to be carrying any documents with him on those occasions? Had she ever witnessed any meeting or encounters, however accidental, between her husband and any strangers? How often did he work in his office at home? Was he a keen photographer? Did he develop his own films?

The questioning shifted to the burning of the notebook. How did she destroy it? Did she set light to the book all at once, or did she burn the pages one by one? What were the flames like? Was there a lot of smoke and of what colour? How long did the operation take?

It was then that they told her that forensic tests had been carried out overnight on the ashes and the scraps of unsinged paper they had collected in order to examine woodpulp fibres, the starch and additives used, and the ink. These tests had established that the material she had destroyed consisted mostly of newspaper and a few sheets of other kinds of paper. Of the latter, no more than one or two sheets could have come from the notebook. *This implied therefore that contrary to her statements, the notebook had not been destroyed.* In that cold room in the middle of winter she broke out into a sweat and could feel it trickle down the middle of her back.

'Of the two or three sheets other than newspaper that you burned, two were manufactured before 1970, and the third in the 1980s. The ink on the older papers was a form of blue dye manufactured in the early Seventies. That on the third sheet had in it pink and mauve dyes of a kind only used in recent years.'

She was being sucked into a trap. They wanted her to confess. Trying to keep her nerve and not break down was the most difficult thing she had ever done in her life.

It was not clear, they said, whether, in the absence of the notebook, there was enough evidence to bring charges against her as an accomplice of David George Maitland Ellis. But the suspicions against her were so strong that they would be referred to the Attorney-General. Meanwhile, her passport would be retained and she was to inform them of all her movements. 'You are advised in your own interests to exercise discretion in any comments you might make to the Press or other persons.'

She was released after having been held in custody for sixteen hours. A flash of light hit her in the eye when she stepped out of the police station and she put her arm up in panic to shield her face. The picture which appeared on the front pages of the papers the next day showed a woman hiding like a criminal.

11

At first she thought she was imagining things. She told herself to watch out or she'd soon find herself addressing blank walls, and it would then be but a short step to the little white van. But it was no good: the man was real, he existed. Time and time again she'd catch sight of him zooming past on his motorbike, trailing her – a man in a black helmet and visor with a white skull and crossbones painted on the back of his bomber jacket.

If this was reality it was grotesque. She felt as if she'd stepped into a surreal cartoon where she was the mouse and he, the man on the motorbike, was the cat. After a while the mouse no longer fled terrifiedly at the mere sight of the tomcat, but learned to venture out, to poke out its nose and sniff. The shadow was liable to disappear down a line of traffic or round a corner as soon as she'd spotted him. Yet she could not shake him off: sooner or later he'd pick up the trail and she'd turn to see him racing past before disappearing in the distance. Sometimes, late in the afternoon when it was already dark, she'd drive down Highgate Hill to see whether he was still around, whether he kept to particular hours. On one of those occasions, as she was waiting for the lights to turn at the crossroads in Parliament Hill Fields, the car behind her bumped and rammed her so that she had to cling dodgem-like to the wheel. This was a more vicious character. When the lights turned, she escaped.

On several occasions she'd returned home to find odd signs of disturbance in the house, and although nothing was missing, although there was no sign of a break-in, odd things were not where she had left them. She also noticed that her letters invariably arrived a day late, the back flaps faintly dog-eared as if other hands had already opened them and gone through the contents.

She no longer knew what was real and what wasn't. One night she noticed a light tapping noise which she took at first for the sound of rain, except that it wasn't raining. When she called the police they found nothing and told her to put it down to an animal in the garden or the shuffling of leaves. On another occasion she woke up on hearing an intruder in her room and sat up in bed to find herself alone. And there were also the nights when nothing happened and she would lie awake and on edge, disconnected thoughts turning to terror in her tired mind.

She left the house less and less frequently, and if she did, it was only to catch a bus to the Broadway in Crouch End. To Angela, this was a comfortingly neutral limbo where she felt anonymous and safe. And then one day, when she was waiting to cross the road by the clock tower, the man on the motorbike sped past her. She crossed the road to Topsfield Parade, her brain beating a dull tomtom inside her head. The world threatened to wrap itself in plateglass around her. She called at a newsagent's to buy a paper and froze as she handed her coins to the woman at the till. The date was unmistakable. Tuesday 28 February. On this day, David would have been fifty. As she walked down Topsfield Parade she felt herself borne along in a procession of ghosts. It was all over. She had not been there to help him when he needed help, and he had never thought of telling her what he was doing or why. The time they had spent together had slipped away, sloughed off like an old skin, but she was, she still was, this miserable woman who was too scared to see things for what they were.

Someone was trying to terrify her. Whether it was one lot or the other she didn't know. But she would make it her business to find out. Like a clockwork mouse, she would wind up in herself the strength to find out who and what the watcher was. She'd corner him. She'd note his registration number and report him to the police.

But what if he was the police? Was she still within the protection of the law?

Everything became more manageable when reduced to the dimensions of a cartoon. One early afternoon, as she was driving towards the Archway Road, she caught sight of the watcher in her rear-view mirror, and it was the mouse that engineered the ambush. As he was gathering speed, ready to overtake her, she veered sharply to the right to obstruct his passage and his machine careered out of control and headed for the pavement opposite where it got stuck in a hedge.

I could have killed him, she thought, horrified at her own actions. She got out of her car and rushed to the man, who was hanging on to the hedge with one hand, pushing the visor off his face with the other. The motorbike was hanging over a walled courtyard some fifteen feet below in a basement. 'Pull me back. Pull me back, you bloody bitch,' he said. The accent was unmistakably South London. Our lot, our bloody lot, she thought as she pulled him back with both arms whilst he pushed with hands and feet. At last the motorbike rolled back onto firm ground. He was safe now. They stared silently at each other. He was thickset with a square jaw and low forehead and his hair was close-cropped like a private's. Car horns screamed around them. 'Get your car out of the way before they charge you with obstruction,' he said.

When she got back into her car she saw him start his motorbike and drive off down the hill without looking back.

She followed him down Shepherds Hill. Not long ago she'd driven the same way in Alice's Mini, the notebook at her side. She'd wanted to destroy it but simply couldn't bring herself to do it. Some deep but obscure urge, patriotism perhaps, had prevented her from doing away with something which, however crazily, might constitute evidence relevant to national security. And since she couldn't hand in the notebook either, she'd dodged the issue by hiding it and pretending to have destroyed it. But the irony was that if the notebook were now to be found, she might be unable to prove her innocence. Her one mistake, she now realized, was to have removed the notebook out of a kind of vanity, for fear of being made to look an idiot. Chaos had resulted from that one decision. As she turned into Crouch End, she lost sight of the man on the motorbike. She thought she'd got the better of him, but she'd never be free of him and his world. She'd become their target. And she had no one to blame for that situation but herself.

PART TWO
A Sprat to Catch a Mackerel

12

The boy lay on his side, not moving, his body still rigid after an attack of *grand mal*, his face blue, looking at Alice who sat by him, comforting him. If the world had a heart, she thought, you felt it when you cared for little ones like this. The child's blue eyes reminded her of another child, a much younger child she'd seen in a dream the night before. The child in the dream had been Albertina's baby by her second marriage, and in that dream Alice had walked up to the baby's cot and saw that he looked a little like his brother Hugo. But then the baby turned its head and Alice was horrified to see that he had a third eye. The child was monstrous and his mother beside herself with grief. At that point Alice had woken up with a start, unable to understand why she should dream of Albertina after all these years, Albertina who was long dead and would now have been as old as Alice herself, had she lived – old and past any hope of child-bearing.

Old. I am old. You are old, Mother William, you are old. And yet you incessantly stand on your head. Do you think, at your age, it is right?

She could not help it. She no longer saw people as they were, but as they had been. When she tried to picture David – and it took some trying – the face she saw was that of the boy David, the pale, wistful face of a tall, fair child with round, blue eyes that gazed at her reproachfully. That other David, the man of importance, she saw only as a grey man, and in her mind that picture became confused with another, that of the Apostle, shortly before his death from a heart attack after he came under suspicion in the aftermath of the Burgess and Maclean scandal.

The Apostle who lived in her memory was altogether different – a fresh-faced young man with black hair and deepset eyes who'd taken her on hunger marches and in whose rooms, daringly unchaperoned, Alice would have tea and listen to Mozart on the gramophone. She became a Marxist out of love, as a gesture of solidarity with the Apostle; her politics owed more to friendship than ideology. She could never quite still her scepticism, her dislike of the indigestibility of Marx's writings; and she put that down to the fact that she lacked depth and intellect and that, as a woman, she could not commit herself to a cause as deeply as the men of her generation. In much the same way, she blamed herself a little when, in the aftermath of the 1937 Moscow show-trials, she smiled and said no. She never actually tore up her green card or resigned from the party. She just dropped out gradually after the Soviet-Nazi Pact, after Finland. The Apostle never wavered but she did not care to know whether he had betrayed or was betrayed. That, somehow, seemed irrelevant to her. If the naïve fantasy of turning the world into a better place had turned into a grotesque nightmare for so many of her contemporaries, the fault, as she saw it, lay in the twists and turns of time and history which had brought evil out of so much youthful idealism. She thought of her Apostle, as she came to think of David, as a victim of circumstance.

Holly Place was part of Alice's life. She had inherited the house shortly before the outbreak of the Second World War, and when she first saw it standing above the valley, like an island amidst a sea of corn, it seemed to spell permanence and hope in the world to come after the war. The house was set on top of a hill not far from Newbury, above a valley where a small village nestled on the edge of a common. A farm, Holly Farm, had originally stood on the site and then, at the turn of the century, Samuel Maitland had commissioned Edwin Lutyens to build him a country house. The Lutyens house was built of a mixture of red and grey-blue brick in the William and Mary style with a double-volume hall. Alice moved down to Holly Place at the beginning of the war. Sara, her sister-in-law, joined her there with her son David. And Albertina came with Sara.

The months that followed were filled with despair. Albertina, who had too freely expressed her admiration for Mussolini, was interned as an alien, leaving her son, Hugo, at Holly Place. In August 1940, Hugo's father was killed in action when his plane was shot down over the Channel. A month later, David's father, also a Fighter Command pilot, died in combat over Maidstone. A telegram arrived. It said, 'Regret to inform you your husband killed. Letter follows.' Two days later Sara was found dead in her bath, her wrists slashed.

Alice became the boys' guardian. There was no time for despair. The farm had been graded 'C' and Alice was told that it would be taken away from her to be farmed by the War Executive Committee in the national interest. She knew she could not allow that to happen. She was granted a year's extension and in that time she worked on the farm with the help of three landgirls, until they won through and the farm was reclassified 'A' the following year.

David went to Eton as his father had planned, and Alice decided that Hugo should go as well. After the war, she turned Holly Place into a special school for multi-handicapped children. The farmland was sold off and a new wing was built as an extension to the Lutyens house. She became the school's first headmistress and continued living in a cottage in the grounds after she retired. She wondered now whether setting up the school had deprived David and Hugo of any semblance of a normal family life, of roots and security.

The hand she held in hers was shaking her gently. The boy sat up and smiled. He had come through. She had given so much of herself to the school that there was little left for those other children who had seemed so strong and so able to look after themselves. She had neglected them.

She made her way to the door, and as she did so children came running to her. She knew each one by name. She loved them all. She walked down the path and into her cottage. She looked out of the window. It was a sunny morning in March and a pale sun lay low on the horizon, shining through a skeleton of bare branches, turning the moisture drops on the window pane to crystal. She heard quick steps on the path and saw Hugo. Something in her quickened and revived, as it always did when Hugo came home. He was hers; the child the Apostle had never given her. He opened the door and let himself in and she saw, in the grey-haired man, the mischievous boy with curly black hair and smiling brown eyes who had elected to stay with her when his mother returned to Italy after the end of the war.

'Is Angela coming?' he asked quickly, and when she nodded, he went on, 'Alice, do me one more favour. Make sure she stays long enough to give me a lift back after the Governors' meeting.' He was Chairman of the Governors. He had reinstated an old tradition whereby a red rose was formally presented to Alice on the school's open day, which was also the focus for its fund-raising activities.

It didn't occur to Alice to question what Hugo was asking her to do, or why.

By the time Angela arrived that afternoon, the weather had turned cold, and angry clouds raced across the darkened sky. Angela wore cream trousers which seemed to float around her body, and her hair was a curious aubergine colour. She nibbled at the food Alice had prepared for her, picking at it with her fork and putting it back again.

'You're not hungry, are you, my dear?' said Alice.

Angela smiled gratefully and pushed her plate away. She rested her elbows on the table and rubbed her face with both hands. 'It's so good to be here. It feels safe.' She looked at Alice. 'Your car,' she said. 'The Mini. It wasn't in the drive . . .'

'It's not here,' said Alice. The poor girl seemed so haggard. Alice wondered again at the meaning of the Mini in Angela's troubled mind. 'It's being serviced. You told me to have it seen to. Do you remember?'

Tears welled up in Angela's eyes.

'It should be back in a day or so,' Alice added lamely. 'Here, my dear, have this.' She handed Angela her handkerchief. 'I have not used it . . .' Women these days no longer seemed to carry a handkerchief. 'Hugo is here today,' she said as lightly as possible. 'He asks if you would be so kind as to give him a lift back into town.'

The tears rolled down Angela's cheeks. 'That is why you asked me here today, isn't it?' she asked accusingly. 'Because of Hugo.'

Alice nodded helplessly and watched as Angela, head bent, held the handkerchief pressed to her face. What have I done to her? wondered Alice. Have I let her down somehow? You are old, Mother William, she thought again. And now that you're perfectly sure you have no brain, why you can stand on your head again and again.

13

'That school is the most important thing in Alice's life,' said Hugo as he and Angela were driving away from Alice's cottage. 'It is her life's work. Her bit for society.'

'Really, you mustn't exaggerate,' said Angela. He hadn't changed, she thought. Hyperbole had always been his natural mode. And now he was going over the top in praising Alice, no doubt because he knew that Angela had felt let down by her.

'How little you know Alice,' he said gently. 'I don't think I'm being sentimental – far from it – a lot of arrogance goes into doing good to humanity. And ruthlessness too. In fact one of my earliest recollections of Alice is of her killing rabbits.'

They were driving along a narrow, winding country lane and were approaching a bend in the road. 'You're having me on,' Angela said. Taking the mickey out of her had been fair game to him and David in the past.

'Having you on,' he repeated. 'What kind of an expression is that?' Briefly their eyes met. She looked away. 'It was during the war,' he said, 'and the wretched creatures had practically taken over the farm. I can picture Alice now, sweat pouring from her as she pursued the miserable beasts, chasing them as they darted between strips of corn, desperate to escape, and then badgering them to death. David and I would run after her screaming, trying to drag her away, but she was unrelenting. Even the landgirls, strapping women that they were, felt sick. It was the kind of awfulness that sticks in the mind and goes on haunting you long after . . . So you see, I have no illusions where Alice is concerned, but I love her for that relentless pursuit of her duty, or what she construes as her duty, which sometimes happens to coincide with what she wants.'

Angela felt he had forgotten her. And then, without warning, he went on. 'David was like that too.' He looked at her. 'I miss him more than I can say,' he said very quietly.

She wasn't prepared for that. The colour rose to her face and old resentments gripped her. She could not trust herself to speak. He laughed as if he could read her thoughts. 'Of course we went on seeing each other. Afterwards. Hardly a week went by without our meeting for lunch or a drink. But we decided to keep it from our wives – you and my ladies. Women don't understand the friendship of men, do they, Angie?'

'How many years is it since we last met – you and I?' she asked, anxious to change the subject. 'Fifteen?'

'Surely not that long . . .' he said. Uncomfortably, the past infiltrated the present. 'I met this raddled female at a party the other day,' he said, as if looking for a safe subject. 'I realized it was someone I had met in my youth – a girl noted for her beauty, a golden girl and bird of paradise. But her beauty was the beauty of a peach. It had wrinkled and decayed more drastically than I could ever have imagined . . . unlike you.'

She burst out laughing. Her hair had turned mauvish orange, red blotches mottled her skin, and she knew she looked haggard.

'Good bones, that's what it is,' he said, ignoring her.

Briefly, she glanced at him. In a little over twenty-one years he'd become this self-important older man, but try as she might there was no dissolve from this to that other face she'd once loved. And now she wondered what it was he was after.

'Why did you ask Alice to arrange for us to meet at Holly Place?' she asked point-blank.

He laughed but ignored the question. 'If I know Alice's cooking, you must be starving by now,' he said. 'I know a place not far from here that serves a pretty succulent roast beef. Why don't we stop there for dinner?'

It was a small hotel off the beaten track, but as she parked in the courtyard she noticed a police car passing by and was suddenly aware that she had seen a good many police cars since leaving Holly Place.

He steered her to an alcove. The waitress, a buxom blonde, brought them a menu, and Angela watched with wry amusement as he played up to her. His wives had been different from each other but the one thing they had had in common was that they glittered – dazzling women to be shown off to other men.

He was right; the Scottish roast beef was lean and tender and it was served with crunchy potatoes and Yorkshire pudding. She hadn't realized until then how ravenous she was, and she helped herself to a second serving. He said he would drive on the way back and poured her more wine.

'Better?' he asked.

She smiled. She was beginning to feel more relaxed.

'I'm an old-fashioned sentimentalist with a soft spot for rabbits,' he said. 'Let me help you, won't you? After all, we were friends once, weren't we?'

'Does your sympathy extend to moles?' she asked quietly. 'Pretty hideous creatures, moles. One need have no conscience about killing them. They're pests, surely?'

'Not at all,' he said swiftly. 'Just a threatened species. Are you sure you're not thinking of shrews? Also in need

91

of protection. Like wildcats.' He fell silent. 'Listen, Angela, you've pushed your luck to the limit and you've got away with it so far, but you need to change gear. After all, the fact that they've sent a report to the Director of Public Prosecutions . . .'

'Attorney-General,' she corrected.

'It shows they're suspecting you of espionage but are not totally sure of their ground and so are leaving it to him to decide whether a prosecution would be justified . . .'

Angela nodded.

'You'll have them breathing down your neck before long – MI5 and the GRU.'

'GRU?' she queried.

'The *Glavnoe Razvedyvatelnoe Upravlenie*, Soviet military intelligence organization and small brother to the KGB.' He looked at her unemotionally. 'You'll be lucky to get away with your life. You've got to realize that time isn't on your side. There is a time bomb ticking under you. The inquest.'

'Why?' she asked. 'Why is that a time bomb?'

'Because they have to find the notebook before the inquest is resumed. Let's face it, it is the only hard evidence they've got. What else is there they could pin on David? They interrogated him over several months and found nothing. No leads. No confession. No radio traffic. No evidence that he had ever been a Communist or had taken part in any active politics. Nothing. And besides,' he smiled fondly, 'David was a consummate master of the art of concealment.'

He came so near, she felt, so near to saying deception. A consummate master of the art of deception. 'Human beings are ultimately unknowable, aren't they?'

'Speak for yourself,' he said sharply. 'I knew David as

92

I know myself.' He covered his face with both hands and she felt the same resentment of their friendship, the same jealousy as of old.

'And so you think he was a spy?'

'Spy is a nasty word. And yet there are aspects to this case that bear David's mark as clearly as a signature.' He laughed. 'Using your notebook, for instance. It's precisely the kind of trick he'd play.'

'When did you last see him?' she asked Hugo.

'David? Oh, I don't know . . . shortly before Christmas, I think. We went for a drink together. He was cheerful. He reckoned that MI5 had decided to drop the matter. It was clear by then that they had no firm basis for a prosecution. And then the bloody CIA went and fed the story to the CBS and bounced MI5 back into the fray. But they reckoned without fate, destiny, or perhaps David himself, if he got wind of the story . . .'

'You mean he was tipped off?' She remembered the scene at the airport, the stranger in the pinstripe suit.

'Possibly, but by whom?'

It was clear to Angela that although David appeared to have taken Hugo into his confidence, he knew nothing of David's clandestine first return to London in January. And she wondered to herself why he should be offering to help her. She caught him looking at her.

'You don't think I'm an MI5 plant, do you? A watcher or *agent provocateur*? Or even perhaps another spy? After all, you might think to yourself, what better cover than that of hell-raising blimp to escape detection?' He smiled. 'Forget it, petal. My only reason for wanting to be your friend is that I have a soft spot for defenceless rabbits.' He reached across the table and grasped her hand. 'And besides, I knew you first, didn't I?'

* * *

93

When they were ready to leave she stood back and watched as he swept his hand under the body of the car and round the inside of each wheel arch. She allowed herself a small thin smile until she saw him unclamp an object from one of the wheel arches. It was a car-tracking device.

'Who could possibly have put it there?' she asked. The device had been fixed to the car by a magnet and contained some small batteries.

'Well, let me put it like this – they're manufactured for one kind of client only, the type that comes in a dark-blue uniform.'

And now, once again, she felt overcome by a feeling of fear. When Hugo offered to come the next day and sniff out any bugs that might have been placed in her home, she agreed, too weary to argue with him. He drove on the way back while she pretended to sleep. When they reached Fitzroy Park, he phoned for a taxi and left.

14

She was still in her dressing gown when Hugo turned up again after lunch the next day. He had a large black bag with him which he carried into the house. He put it down and then stood and looked around him at the piano, the pictures, the books on the shelves, objects which had belonged to David and now objectified his presence. He turned to Angela. Uncomfortably, she tightened the belt of her dressing gown round her waist.

'What's wrong?' he asked softly as if afraid he might be overheard. 'They've put the frighteners on you, have they?'

'They're searching Holly Place,' she said. 'Alice phoned earlier to say so. She'll ring back when they've done.'

He put his arms around her and laid her head on his shoulder. 'Don't worry, petal. I'm here to look after you.'

How tempting, she thought, how tempting to have someone to rely on, to let Hugo help her.

He emptied the bag's contents and placed them neatly on the floor – a black box, a radio set, a rod. 'A counter-surveillance receiver,' he said in a low voice. He switched on the device, which emitted a curious sound half-way between radio interference and a vacuum cleaner. He swept round the room with the rod, and the signals became louder when he reached the skirting board. He stopped. He found a first bug inside a plug adaptor, another behind the piano, a third inside the TV set. He took them to pieces. One contained a tiny microphone, a miniaturized transmitter, and a small battery. The one inside the TV set was a camera with a pin-hole lens pointing at the room. Every new find delighted Hugo as much as it horrified Angela.

'Listen, old girl, there's no point in you hanging around, is there? Go and smarten up a bit. I'll give you a shout when I've finished. And then we can talk.'

She walked up the stairs on quivering legs and ran to the bathroom, where she was sick. As she washed the vomit away and wiped her face she saw the pitiful reflection of a terrified woman in the glass, and fear surged within her. She went to her room and lay on her bed listening to the buzz of the electronic sweeper as it moved from one room to another. At this very moment, Special Branch were also searching Holly Place. What would they find?

Eventually, she heard Hugo switch off the sweeper and went to join him. He was sitting down on the floor loading up the listening devices in his black bag. 'Well, we've snoopered the snoopers.'

'Where did you get hold of this clobber?' she asked.

He tapped his nose without answering.

'And how did you know how it works?'

'I was taught by masters,' he said. 'Look at this little beauty.' It was a piece of equipment with a tiny tape recorder inside it. 'Your run-of-the-mill transmitters will only transmit a short distance – say, to a van down the road. This object will pick up quite a lot but it cannot transmit it automatically. It's got to be retrieved – by someone breaking in when the house is empty for instance.'

'Is it legal?'

He shrugged. 'What would they be guilty of? At most transmitting without a licence. And besides, rabbit, you're a potential subversive and the least you'd expect them to do is keep you under surveillance. It's their job. Defending the realm and all that.'

'They?'

'Our lot. The Security Service and their legmen in Special Branch. It's all covered by royal warrant, official warrants and fancy names like Azure, Phidias and Tinkerbell – MI5 jargon for bugging, mail intercepts and telephone bugs.'

'And the other lot?' she asked.

'Much nastier,' he said. 'Given to killing off turbulent people like you with poisoned umbrella tips.' He packed the equipment away in the black bag. 'It's my head as well as yours above the parapet now.'

She nodded helplessly. And he a Member of Parliament. Why was he taking such risks? Was he really just wanting to help her?

'Listen,' he said. 'Has it never occurred to you that perhaps David did not jump but was pushed, and that the same could happen to you? Dead women don't talk.'

It sounded like a threat. 'What do you want, Hugo?' she asked.

'The notebook,' he said simply.

She was momentarily speechless. Was that all his offer of friendship amounted to?

'What do you want to do with it?' she asked.

'I can't tell you.'

She shook her head. She could not let him have the notebook. If he worked for MI5, the notebook might be taken as evidence against her as well as David; and if it was the Russians he worked for, then she wanted nothing to do with him.

He slapped her. His face distorted with anger, he slapped her again and again and again, as if trying to batter her into submission. He stopped when the telephone rang. 'That will be Alice,' he said.

Angela touched her bloodied mouth where the teeth had torn the skin and then looked at her fingers. She rubbed them together, almost surprised to see so much blood.

'Perhaps I'd better take it,' he said. This violence was unlike him, but as she gazed at him a stillness came over his face, a stillness like a mask that gave nothing away.

'No,' she said. 'I'll get it.'

Alice told her that the police had left, and as she put the phone down and turned to Hugo she was unable to hide the relief she felt.

He stood there, observing her calmly and detachedly, revealing nothing. 'Holly Place is clear?' he asked.

She nodded. 'Yes. They found nothing.'

'There was no reason to worry then, was there? – unless there was something you expected them to find, that is.'

15

When Hugo phoned Fanny's hall of residence to invite her out for a meal the following Saturday at some coffee place in London, she agreed so readily that he was taken aback. Fanny herself made two concessions for the occasion – she borrowed a dress from a friend and she travelled down by rail.

As they were walking down Pall Mall she wondered whether they were going in the right direction. She had pictured a vaguely Italian coffee place with cream cakes and foamy cappuccino – the kind of place to which someone like Hugo could comfortably take a scruffy niece. She felt disoriented when he motioned her up some steps and she found herself walking past the lamp standards, through the lobby and into the atrium saloon of the Reform Club. It was a vast room, surrounded by colonnaded galleries on two floors under a glass-domed skylight. She gazed silently at the colonnades of marble and granite, the paintings on the wall, the marble busts, the mosaic floors.

'Not exactly a Tory haunt,' said Hugo, 'but I've been a member since my early days as a journalist. What do you think of it?'

She didn't wish to appear overawed. 'Victorian plush,' she said briefly.

'Early Victorian, actually. Built in 1830 by Charles Barry in the style of the Italian Renaissance Palazzo.'

'A throwback to a time when half the world was coloured red on the map . . .'

He laughed. They walked to the coffee room on the ground floor and Fanny felt she was penetrating a strange world of spaces mysteriously contained within other spaces, where rooms had coffered ceilings framed by Ionic columns and where, notwithstanding the mirrors all around, there was an atmosphere of privacy. She saw herself reflected in a glass – a plain girl in white, a girl engineer, faintly ridiculous.

'You look sexy,' he said, as if reading her thoughts.

She felt a surge of joy. Then she thought, I shouldn't be pleased at this kind of patronizing rubbish. She shook her head. 'Sally is the pretty one. I'm the plain sister.'

'Not plain at all. A today girl full of can-do. Particularly in those leather pants you wore at the House.' He was relaxed, friendly, amused.

In spite of herself Fanny smiled. Would she dare? She dared. 'You're not bad looking yourself,' she said, her head cocked to one side. 'In a slightly rouéish way, perhaps?'

He seemed a little discomfited and then laughed. 'I can remember you in nappies, Miss Fanny. Listen. Stop fighting me. Tell me what you've been doing with yourself since we last met.'

'Mugging up espionage.'

'Have you learned a lot?'

'Nothing that matters.'

'Tell me,' he said.

'The nearest equivalent is a game of Spot the Bluff. Or Counter-Bluff.' Why was it so easy to talk to Hugo when she had found it so difficult to talk to her father? Fanny felt she was getting in her stride at last. 'I was left wondering whether the man who named my father was really a defector, or whether he was a plant, a disinformation agent, a double agent or even a discard.'

'The man Poliakin?'

She nodded. 'This game that men play with its dirty tricks and silly pranks seems to have pretty little of any value coming out of it.'

'Women too, surely?' he said. 'There are women too in this game, aren't there?'

'They're more often the bait. But I'm not making a feminist point. As a species, the spy seems much the same whether he comes in the Soviet or Western variety. There is this curious symmetry throughout. Point and counterpoint. Our traitors are their heroic internationalists. Their traitors are our brave agents working clandestinely for peace. Each side claims virtue for itself and evil for the enemy. Each side is so uniquely concerned with the threat posed by the enemy that it is blind to the threat it poses them.'

'Aren't you a bit harsh? Spies are the unofficial diplomatists of the cold peace. A way for each side to understand the other – to acquire and analyse intelligence about the other's position, its negotiating and sticking points. And perhaps treachery is not altogether inglorious if it can also be presented as a tool of politics . . .'

'And the traitor?' she asked.

'The traitor is alone. Call yourself an agent and you're respectable. Call yourself a traitor and the gates of hell open up before you.' She was surprised at his bitterness.

'Anyhow,' she said. 'Anyhow. None of all this seems to ring any bells with what my father was.'

'And that is why you agreed to come to dinner with an old roué like me? You want us to talk about David?'

She nodded.

'I'll tell you everything I know,' he said. 'But I'll expect something from you in return. Is that a deal?'

* * *

As they were leaving, he took her before a fireplace surmounted by a mirror. 'Look,' he said. She gazed in the mirror, but there was no reflection. It was as if she had become invisible. The effect was surreal.

She understood at once. Two marble busts had been placed back to back on each side of a pane of plain glass to create the illusion of a mirror. There was no mirror. And hence, no reflection. 'Beware Fanny, you are surrounded by illusion.'

'And you,' he asked when they were in the car. 'Have you never felt the pull of Communism?'

She thought of the Gulags, Hungary, Czechoslovakia, Poland and Afghanistan. 'No, never,' she said.

'But they're a lot of lefties, your generation, aren't they?'

'They care about jobs mostly, my lot. And things like peace, race, ecology and pollution. None of these things embraces a total ideological theory. And besides, ideology is a largely discredited concept.'

He lived in a Regency terrace near Holland Park, and although the house had been newly painted on the outside it was shabby, almost seedy, inside. It was furnished in an art nouveau style which must have been attractive when new, but the cream and white decor had become worn and dingy. Hugo passed the matter off lightly. 'The place needs a fresh coat of paint, but all that must take second place to maintaining my ex-lady-wives in the style to which I can no longer aspire myself.'

What were they like, she asked, his ex-es?

'The first one ran off with a ballet dancer. The second was neurotic. Bloody women. You're all the same, aren't you?' He turned on a table lamp in the form of Diana the

102

huntress holding up a pink globe. 'There. It looks better like this, doesn't it?'

Through the open curtains the deserted street gleamed darkly in the shadowless night. Fanny noticed two photographs in silver frames on the mantelpiece. One showed a blonde and reed-slim Alice in a white silk dress and wide-brimmed straw hat, the other a young couple. The man was in uniform and the girl, dark and pretty, wore a cotton frock.

'My parents,' said Hugo. 'I'm not a born nob like you.' He dismissed her protests. 'Your family's relation to mine was always an upstairs-downstairs affair.'

Hugo's father had been her grandfather's butler and both men were reservists who had trained in auxiliary squadrons. When the war broke out, they joined the RAF and became squadron pilots. David's father was a commissioned officer, Hugo's a direct entry NCO. Both men were killed at about the same time during the war.

'And your mother?'

'My mother was the cook. She was Italian and was interned shortly after my father died in action. I was not yet seven at the time. After the war she went back to Italy, where she was to die a few years later, and I opted to stay with Alice. It was the worst possible betrayal. "In the lost childhood of Judas, Christ was betrayed." Do you know who said that?'

She shook her head. 'Were you very unhappy as a child?'

'On the contrary,' he said. 'In spite of everything, my childhood was very happy. David and I were bound together like the fingers of one hand.' He took a small snapshot out of his wallet and showed it to her. Two boys of seven or eight in grey flannel shorts, their grey woollen socks falling down round their ankles, their caps not quite

103

straight on their heads. Hugo and David. Although a little younger, David was always ahead. His father had put his name down for Eton, and it was Alice's idea of equality that he, Hugo, should go too. Oddly enough, Hugo got beaten rather a lot but loved Eton, whereas David, on whom he could always rely then and later to pull his chestnuts out of the fire, David had hated Eton. He was extremely clever and managed to bag most of the prizes but he deeply resented Eton's hierarchical society, the privileges of the senior boys, their harsh discipline, the arrogance of the wealthier boys. He'd felt stifled by Eton.

'Do you think my father was a Communist?'

'Not overtly. He was an idealist. I don't think he ever really liked the poor – or understood them – but he hated privilege and inequality. And yet, ironically, he was something of a snob. An intellectual snob, if you like. He could be very contemptuous of people who did not measure up to his standards. On the whole, I think he was more interested in ideas than people. The most important influence in his life was that of a man who had been a friend of Alice's at Cambridge in the Thirties and became the victim of a witch-hunt in the early Fifties. I sometimes wonder whether this man did not recruit David even before he left Eton. He died when David and I were about eighteen.'

A silence hung between them. 'Did my father talk to you about any espionage activities he was involved in?'

'I was aware, because he'd told me so, that David was engaged in some kind of espionage since about 1982, but the impression he gave me was that these activities were arranged in connivance with MI5 and that the information he passed over was either duff or published stuff.'

'Are you sure? You're not indulging me, are you?' Relief flooded within her. He had done nothing wrong.

Her father had remained true to his principles. Let it be so. Please let it be so. She tried to think rationally. 'What kind of information did he pass over?'

'Amongst other things, information on the nature and extent of the US assistance we got during the Falklands.'

Although it was well known that the US helped with fuel and some weapons, very little was known about the intelligence gathered from the US, including data collected by spy satellites.

'All this could only be damaging, couldn't it?'

A shadow passed. He looked at her sharply, his face suddenly impenetrable. 'Not if it was disinformation,' he said. There was a full moon in the sky outside and the sky itself was indigo-blue and seemed translucent. After a while, Hugo broke the silence. 'I feel sure that David would never have given away anything that might even remotely damage national security.'

Could she trust him? Was he telling her the truth? Did he himself know the truth?

'Something is worrying you?' he asked.

'I was just thinking how strange it was that you were so much in my father's confidence . . .' If David had indeed been involved in espionage would he have spoken so openly to Hugo?

Hugo's eyes narrowed to slits in his face.

'I'm naturally suspicious,' she said apologetically. 'After all, I was a would-be arsonist as a child. It nearly wrecked my parents' marriage.'

'Not at all,' he said quickly, absentmindedly, as if attending to something else. 'It salvaged it.'

It hurt, thought Fanny, it actually hurt, that muscle, her heart.

'You went through an assessment procedure which your father challenged, on Alice's advice, because it was made by a psychologist and not, as it was supposed to be, by a doctor. When a doctor and a psychiatrist subsequently examined you they said you had been trying to draw attention to yourself to shore up your parents' marriage.' He got up and switched off the lights. The sky was now pale blue and streaked with lilac clouds. The moon had faded. The sun was a bobble of molten gold. A new day was beginning to dawn. Hugo kissed her lightly on the lips. 'I am an old roué. I kiss all the girls,' he said, 'and their mums too.'

She still felt it, that pain in the region of the heart. 'And Tom,' she asked quietly before his blank stare. 'Tom is your son, isn't he?'

16

Wednesday 4 April. Fanny lay wide awake at four in the morning, too cold and too stiff to sleep, and although she wore all her day clothes and an anorak, the damp from the wet ground underneath still seemed to penetrate through her sleeping bag and every layer of clothing, chilling her to the bone. Her head ached and her eyes were smarting from the smoke of camp fires. She curled up and tried to rub some warmth in her toes, which had become numb. It was her fourth night at Greenham. The women were to have been evicted two days before to make way for a road-widening scheme at the gates of the missile base. But Monday and then Tuesday came and nothing happened, nothing but the comings and goings of visitors of various sorts, supporters, Press people, irate locals – 'ratepayers' – who all went back home to their warm beds when the protesters returned to their tents and polythene benders in the junkyard that was the Greenham Women's Peace Camp.

Here, more than a year before, she'd watched from a hiding place inside a bender as David waded through the mud, looking for her. He'd asked after her, and two girls wearing chains round their necks had kissed each other on the lips without answering him. Then David went on striding over the muddy no-man's-land of the peace camp. It was that David she remembered now – a man of integrity, unsullied by suspicion, a man who'd always lived by the rules.

Fanny tossed and turned in her sleeping bag. Hugo had

told her he was convinced that Angela had hidden the notebook in the cottage at Holly Place, and his brief to her was clear. Be unobtrusive, he'd told her. Call at Greenham Common first, and then make your way to Holly Place. Don't tell Alice what you're doing, but find out what places have been searched by the police and skip these. See if Alice has any clues about hiding places. Above all, drop everything if you are trailed. Only get in touch if you've found the notebook.

But now, the quest for papers that might incriminate her father seemed like an insane adventure. No earthly good could come out of it. If MI5 had been in league with her father, they already knew what was in the notebook. And so did the enemy know what information he'd given them. The notebook was cold potatoes. This was a game played by spooks and shadows where nothing was what it seemed, where everything was double-cross and double-dealing, and where the people who got hurt in the end weren't the spooks but poor blighters like her father. Let them stew in their foul mess. She would have nothing to do with it. She would be nobody's stooge.

She heard the distant rumble of a car in the distance, followed by women's screams, and she knew that the bailiffs had arrived.

She stepped out of her tent and saw dozens, hundreds of policemen standing shoulder to shoulder, forming a cordon round the camp whilst the women, still heavy with sleep, scrambled around the benders removing their pots and pans, bags, clothes and prams before the bailiffs could get to them. The air was full of cries, and as they shouted and screamed at the men someone started the witches' song, and then others joined in until the women's alarm turned to laughter and defiance as the heavy, clumsy men attacked the flimsy edifice of tents and

108

benders. And now the women themselves set fire to their possessions and Fanny shouted and screamed with them as she thrust her tent and sleeping bag in the middle of the fire and watched tall flames shoot up in the cold morning air.

17

Friday 13 April. Outside Waterloo Station a small crowd had formed around two punks who were fighting sprawled out on the ground. The man on top, blood streaming from his eye, held the other pinned down, vengefully shaking him by the shoulders so that his head hit the ground time and time again. When a trickle of blood stained his hair there was a gasp in the crowd but no one moved. Some other punks stood around, crazy smiles on their faces. Angela stepped forward and stood above the men. The attacker looked up at her, and the blood lust in his bloodied eye sickened her. She was scared of being sucked into a violence she could not withstand. She drew back.

It was, she felt, an act of cowardice. But then, what could she have done? The thought of her weakness preyed on her as she crossed the Jubilee Gardens to the South Bank where she could see Hugo waiting for her. He was leaning over the parapet by the Thames, staring at the Houses of Parliament across the water.

'There was something I wanted to tell you,' he said brusquely without looking at her, 'which is why I phoned this morning.'

Briskly he walked ahead and she followed him down Sovereign's Walk, past the Jubilee Gardens, past the Festival Hall where the GLC had erected itself a pink and white birthday cake, past the bookstalls outside the National Film Theatre, past the National Theatre where a structure like a small arena was being sculpted from rock-like blocks of stone – 'What do you think is going to happen to us by the time this is finished?' he asked – and they kept walking till they came to a point where the promenade was boarded up and they could go no further.

Hugo sat down on a wooden bench, and as she sat next to him he began telling her of his journey to Moscow and Ivanov's threat on her life. The sound of his voice mingled with the cries of seagulls flying over the Thames. She heard him say that the Soviets had a hold over him but it wasn't espionage; that David had been a double agent run by MI5; that the notebook contained coded information about David's assignations and the documents he'd passed over; that the Soviets wanted to check that information to see whether it was genuine. He himself felt that no harm would probably come from that since it seemed clear that David had fed the GRU nothing but disinformation. However it seemed sensible that they should both examine the notebook together to arrive at some kind of decision.

Incongruous images of punks fighting in Red Square formed in Angela's mind. She shook her head. No, she said. Even if she had the notebook – which she didn't – she would never consider releasing it to the Soviets, and that was final.

'I rather thought you'd say that,' he said. 'So be it. It's your life. I wash my hands of all this.' He looked at her. 'Why didn't you tell me about Tom?' he asked gently.

If only he'd been angry, she might have known then what to say. As it was, she had no explanation and no excuse.

'I'll have to tell them,' he said, as he was turning to leave.

She nodded. 'I understand,' she said.

He was to draw a chalk circle on a plane tree in Kensington as a code to indicate that he hadn't managed

111

to get the notebook. With any luck, they might even assume it had been destroyed.

And if not?

He shrugged. Hitmen sharpening knives in dark corners. Who knew? 'Be careful,' he said. 'Take care.'

The South Bank was filling up with lunchtime crowds of office workers. Two joggers came running up to the end of the promenade and then started running back again.

In the distance, the rumble of traffic on the north bank was like a heart beat.

She remembered Hugo saying, 'Be careful,' when, a few days later, she saw in the rear-view mirror of David's Jaguar a woman on the pavement behind her gesturing wildly and pointing to something under the car. Angela could not hear what the woman was saying but she instinctively pressed the clutch, switched into neutral and jumped out.

She fell heavily on her hands and knees and felt foolish until she heard the woman scream that there was a bomb under the car, and then she picked herself up and ran as fast as her legs could carry her.

The car rolled forward a few yards before the bomb went off. People screamed as flames shot out and the windscreen and roof blew out, scattering blazing debris over the street and pavements.

The woman who'd spotted the booby-trap bomb had disappeared, vanishing in the crowd. As Angela stood staring at the blazing wreckage of the car, she understood.

It was the beginning of the countdown.

18

19 April. Maundy Thursday. The yellow Mini drove up to the top of the multi-storey car park at the Brent Cross shopping centre. A woman with a bandaged hand emerged and waved to a man in a grey suit who was standing by the lift door.

'You're late,' he said.

'Alice was delayed and I had to wait for her to arrive before I could come and join you. With my left hand in the state it is it was as much as I could do to drive here. You'll have to dig up the notebook yourself . . . It's hidden under the back seat of the Mini.'

She watched detachedly as he scrambled in to the back of the narrow car, crouched in the tiny space between the back and front seats, pulled off the cushion, turned it upside down, and slipped his arm under the plastic cover to bring out the trophy, the evidence, the exhibit, the booby prize – a crumpled cardboard folder inscribed with the words 'Angela's Effusions'.

'Rum business, this,' he said as he extricated himself from the back. They sat side by side in the front of the old Mini in a North London car park and started leafing through the pages of a student notebook covered in a spidery scrawl that was underscored throughout with a series of tiny dots. Could these insignificant blots really hold dangerous secrets?

Hugo flicked over a few pages and burst out laughing. 'Guff,' he said. 'Pure guff. All frills and cadenza and not a sensible thought anywhere. Funny sort of apple on which to change the rules of motion.'

Hogwash more like, she thought bitterly. Humbug. Moonshine. Illusion. My romantic dirty linen washed in public.

'Listen, don't take it all so personally.'

'It's my life and my bloody neck,' she said. Ridicule added to injury. The ultimate insult. 'Do you know how I have felt these last few days? Cornered. Hounded. A wounded animal waiting for the kill.'

'What tripe you talk . . .' he said, patting her bandaged hand. 'What matters is not what you can see in the wretched book, but what you can't see. Its hidden messages.'

He tackled the incryptions in the notebook with the same excited interest he'd shown before when searching for listening devices. He began by establishing that the dots could not be scratched off and were not therefore microdots, and that there were no indentations on the pages of the notebook that might be taken to indicate the use of secret writing. His hunch, he said, was that the dots were part of a private cipher. The dotted letters were the elements of a secret message written in code. They would need to be translated into other letters to yield a clear message. He suspected that the system was one which David – ever a keen mathematician – had toyed with in the past. It involved the use of two keys. One key was used to write a message *into* the secret language – the text made up of the dotted letters in the notebook. The second key served to read *from* the secret language. There was no other connection between the two keys, but both were based on the factors of a mathematical problem and unless one had the key to decrypt the secret message the code was practically unbreakable, even by using computers or cryptanalysis.

'You mean that this is a code that only David would understand?'

'Unless he chose to give the decrypting key away. Anyone with that key would find it child's play to decode the secret message.'

'And you are assuming that since he was working for MI5 he gave the key to MI5 and not to the KGB and GRU.'

He nodded. 'To the Soviets the secret language would be gobbledegook.' He hesitated. 'The question is have I got it right, and have I got David right?'

Let him decide, she thought. She told Hugo of David's secret return to London, his meeting with the stranger at Heathrow, and the plan which she'd foiled when she removed the notebook from his desk. He was interested but unmoved.

'Let me see the notebook,' she said. She could not judge whether Hugo's reading of the cipher was accurate or merely fanciful, and the blots on the pages of the notebook seemed to her a less likely key than David's motivation in using the notebook to carry his private messages. What could have induced him to act in that way? She searched for an answer in the language of the notebook.

The first entry was dated 25 April 1963 and it wasn't about David at all, but Hugo – the guff that had made him laugh.

I love you. Love you across the unknown years and through my stranger being. Love beyond the ending of my love and the awakening to days without you. I love you stupidly. Stupidly, I love you still.

And then came the time, only six months later, when she was falling in love with David.

Is it love then, this fancy, and if not love, what is it? It's your hand close to mine but not touching. It's me letting you down and you smile. It's you laughing at my jokes. It's looking into your eyes and the world finds its soul.

And later still, in February 1964, after Tom's birth, there was an entry which referred to all three of them – David, Hugo and herself.

A Valentine's Day party at Hugo's in Holland Park. Chat, social chat, small talk, talk. About chamber pots. About ships. About feet. I can find nothing to say about these things. You reach out and say something in my ear and your lips touch my face. Across the room, Hugo is watching us. Hugo and you and me. Angles multiplied through a kaleidoscope. A year ago he and I were lovers. You married me to give his son a name. And now it is you I love. I dream of you and Hugo and me making love together. And to my dream I say, politely, beseechingly, to Hugo: 'Leave us: please leave us alone.'

'What a dirty mind you've got, Angie,' said Hugo, reading over her shoulder. 'Me and David and you making love together? Shades of *The Story of O* . . .'

'Do you realize the notebook is the only evidence there is that Tom is your son?' she said. Wasn't that a more likely key?

'Well what of that?' he asked coldly.

'Isn't it possible that at heart David hated you as he hated me, because he'd saved us from our mistakes and felt trapped?' He was looking at her without flinching. 'What if the notebook is his way of paying us back?'

'A trap?' He gave it not even a moment's thought. 'I don't want to think like that,' he said, and then he started

116

laughing and the hooting, bird-like sound filled the car. 'Mr Mole setting a trap on Mrs Mole and her erstwhile lover?' Tears of merriment filled his eyes. 'My poor Angela, it simply ain't like that, spying. The public and the private event are two separate things. Chalk and cheese. They don't mix. There is no link.'

'Why then should he have used the notebook, of all possible things?'

'For some perfectly sound reason which will no doubt come out in the fullness of time when a new story will emerge, a story that will have nothing to do with your experience or mine and will come to be seen as the true account.'

'Why should it be any truer than what I think and feel?'

'Because spying is about public scandals, not private misfortunes.'

He had been given a telephone number to use if and when he had managed to obtain the notebook and he dialled it from a phone box outside Archway tube station, using agreed code words. 'Can I speak to Mary Kaye?' As he expected, they said it was a wrong number and he hung up. The place of the rendezvous for the handover had also been fixed in advance. That evening, in the vaulted, candlelit cellars of a wine bar by the Thames, he would hand over the notebook inside a copy of the previous Thursday's *Guardian* to a stranger carrying an identical copy of the *Guardian*. And then it would be all over, all over bar the shouting.

'And you,' she said stubbornly, as she dropped him at Holloway station. 'Why did you get involved in this business? Was it merely to help me, or was there something else as well?'

117

He looked very tired suddenly. 'You don't trust me, do you?'

She looked at him. He was right. In her heart of hearts, she didn't altogether trust him, and it wasn't simply because she'd loved him once and he'd spurned her.

'How can I trust you if you won't tell me the truth?' A rictus of pain creased the corners of his mouth and she felt a stab of remorse at her ingratitude. 'Listen,' she said. 'Listen. How can I believe you absolutely? Now you tell me David was a double agent, and yet you started off by implying he was a spy . . .'

'On the way back from Holly Place?' he asked and she nodded. He laughed but the laughter was forced. 'I don't suppose I can blame you,' he said. 'In this game of deception how can anyone be expected to trust anyone else?' He turned away. 'The simple answer to your question is that I did not wholly trust you either. I felt that David's work for MI5 was part of a hidden agenda, privileged information if you like, and I didn't want to break his cover if I could help it. Not even to you.'

'And yet you'd trusted David implicitly?' she asked. But then so had she, hadn't she?

118

19

The crunch came in May, at the time when cherry trees shed their blossom in street gutters, and it came with a brief note in a plain envelope inviting Angela to attend a meeting with security officers to help tie up some loose ends. A set time, date, and place were given for the meeting. No alternatives were suggested and it was clear that none would be considered: the invitation was a summons.

Less than a fortnight before, Hugo had handed her notebook to an unknown stranger in a London wine bar. She wondered now whether that act, in which she was implicated, could have been treasonable – communicating to an enemy information prejudicial to the security of the State? She wondered how much the security services knew.

She didn't try to get in touch with Hugo. She reasoned that they were probably both under surveillance. In truth, she felt a sly, sullen resentment. She was in a mess again, and blamed him for it.

The meeting took place in the MI5 safe house at South Audley Street in circumstances which seemed at first to be normal to the point of banality – four people sitting round a horseshoe-shaped table, a screen stretched out on a wall, a tape recorder before the chairman, and the chairman himself – a short, stocky man who smoked a pipe. He nodded briefly to acknowledge Angela's arrival as she was shown to a place at one end of the horseshoe. The place at the other end was empty. There was an eerie silence in the room and it seemed curiously cut off from the world outside.

For a full ten minutes nothing happened. They waited. Angela watched as the other members of the meeting looked at their watches, looked at one another, or exchanged written messages. There was a tension in the air, a sense of expectancy, but no one spoke and she wondered whether secret microphones had been set in the table to record the meeting. They were waiting for something to happen. Or someone.

And then he arrived, stopped briefly at the entrance of the meeting room and looked straight to the head of the table. The chairman stood up and the two men faced each other like assailants sizing each other up before the fray. They could not have been more different. The short man, compact and self-contained, rock-solid, consciously occupying the moral high ground. The tall man at the door, handsome, florid, striving for effect, theatrical. He was shown to the other end of the horseshoe and pulled the chair away from the table before sitting back, his long legs crossed before him, a man in a tight corner assuming centre stage. He turned to Angela and winked at her.

'If you're quite ready, Mr Gray, perhaps we could now start?' said the chairman in a tone of pained irritation. He had a rather high-pitched voice and spoke in the clear, precise tones of one accustomed to having his pronouncements taken down verbatim. He introduced the proceedings blandly, neutrally. 'Some allegations have been made to the security services over a number of months, and this interrogation provides a means to explore them further and give the person concerned the opportunity to clear himself.'

It was only then that Angela realized that the meeting

was to be an interrogation, that the chairman was the interrogator, and that the suspect was Hugo. How abject, she thought, how abject her relief at that moment. It was Hugo's freedom that was at stake, not hers.

'A set procedure will be followed,' went on the interrogator. 'It will begin with an examination of the early life and career of the person under investigation and then proceed to a more detailed consideration of points of specific concern. The session is likely to go on until 5.30 P.M. with a break for lunch at about 12.30 P.M. Do you have any questions?'

'Why is it necessary for Mrs Maitland Ellis to be here?' asked Hugo calmly.

The interrogator ignored him. They were later to recognize this as one of his ploys – he would ignore statements or questions as a means of unsettling the other person.

'That will be made clear to you at the end of the day,' he said to Angela. His staring eyes betrayed no emotion.

He opened a tagged folder before him – the brief. 'Let us go over the circumstances of your early life, Mr Gray. Your family had close relations with the Maitland Ellises, I believe?' He paused. 'Your father was the butler. Your mother the cook.' Another pause. 'A master/servant relationship, would you say?'

'I wouldn't. But you might . . .'

'Your father was killed during the war. Your mother was interned as an alien and not unnaturally decided to return home to Italy when she was released. You opted to stay in England with your guardian, Alice Maitland Ellis. A year later your mother died. You were how old at the time?'

'Thirteen.'

'Quite. You were at Eton then and in the same house

121

as David Maitland Ellis. He was a bit of a swot – "sap" in Eton parlance, I believe. As for you, your prowess on the playing field won you a measure of acceptance. Popularity, even. But you got caned rather a lot, didn't you?'

There was no comment from Hugo.

'Then, as later, you could rely on Maitland Ellis to pull your chestnuts out of the fire. It was the expression you used, I believe?'

Hugo shrugged. The discussion, he seemed to be implying was being conducted at too crude a level to engage his interest.

The interrogator's voice rose. 'It must have been uncomfortable for a working-class boy to find himself at Eton in the Forties.' It was a statement of fact. 'Did you fit in?' he asked point-blank.

'I think so,' said Hugo smoothly.

'They nicknamed you Jeeves.'

'And look at me now – outnobbing the nobs.'

'Compensating perhaps?'

'Perhaps. And perhaps not . . .'

The interrogator tried another tack. 'Alice Maitland Ellis was a Marxist and you became a Tory?'

'We both chose to betray our class,' said Hugo good-humouredly. 'Though I might add that my Toryism in no way detracts from my sense of obligation to the Maitland Ellises . . .'

The interrogator ignored the remark. He turned to the next page in his brief. 'Would you care to take us over your experiences after you left Eton?'

Hugo spoke of the scholarship he won to Oxford, of his national service with the King's Royal Rifles, of reading history at Trinity College and starting work as a trainee journalist on the *Daily Telegraph*. At about the same time, David had come down from Cambridge, having read mathematics at Trinity College, and was then an Assistant Principal at the Ministry of Defence. They shared a flat.

'You shared other things as well, I believe?'

Hugo looked blank.

'Girls,' said the interrogator. 'You were notorious for taking his girlfriends away from him, I believe?'

Hugo's mocking laughter rang out in the silent room. He said nothing.

'With one exception, you took his girlfriends away from him. And that one exception could perhaps more appropriately come under the rubric of pulling your chestnuts out of the fire . . .'

Briefly, Angela and Hugo glanced at each other. 'Is this washing of dirty linen really necessary?' asked Hugo.

'Perhaps you will let me be the judge of that,' said the interrogator curtly. He seemed rattled. He leafed through his brief. 'I shall go over the remaining ground very quickly,' he said, reading out from the text before him in a flat, toneless voice. 'You first entered Parliament as a result of a by-election in 1965 and lost your marginal seat the following year. You entered Parliament again in June 1970 and retained that seat throughout successive elections, although you have remained on the backbenches. You married for a first time in 1963 and that marriage was dissolved in 1971. Your first wife left you for a defecting Russian ballet dancer and divorced you on the grounds of unreasonable behaviour. A second marriage in 1979 was dissolved a year later and your second wife subsequently suffered a nervous breakdown. You have had to and are continuing to support her. You have had to pay substantial costs arising from both divorces. By 1981 your financial circumstances had become precarious and you became the executive director of a firm engaged in the

123

export of electronic equipment and machine tools.' He paused again. 'Is that a fair summary, would you say, or are there any points of fact you wish to challenge?'

The interrogator sat back in his chair. Angela was conscious, as of a force, of his will being brought to bear against Hugo, to prevail against him.

The picture of Hugo that had emerged from that morning's session reflected the security services' perception of him. They saw him as an outsider, someone who appeared to have made it but who did not really fit in, and whose life and career were marked by a series of misjudgments. In their minds, he was already guilty. Or so it seemed to Angela. They were looking for evidence to confirm an expectation of guilt. Why? she wondered. What did they have against him?

'I might not agree with your gloss,' said Hugo at last, 'but it would be fruitless to challenge your interpretation of the facts.' He sat, shoulders hunched, arms folded defensively before him.

The interrogator snapped his brief shut. 'Well then, since we've reached a natural point of transition, let's call a break for lunch.'

He filled his pipe, lit it and puffed away reflectively as Hugo and Angela stood up and left the room together. The door was shut after them. The others stayed on for a debriefing session.

Angela and Hugo stopped at a pub in a Mayfair backstreet and sat at a small, round table by a window. The building opposite was being pulled down and the world outside looked like a demolition site.

'No polygraph. No truth drugs. No rat-infested cells. They've even let us keep our clothes on. Let's face it, it could have been a lot worse,' she said. It wasn't much of a joke.

124

'The worst of it is that the bastard's right,' said Hugo. 'My twenty years in the monkey house have been nothing but an act – all bluff and bluster and nothing to chalk up at the end of the day. Failure.' He looked at her, through her, not seeing her. 'I could leave tomorrow and it would make not a jot of difference.'

'Tell us about your firm's work,' said the interrogator. His thin voice was steel sharp, a rapier.

Hugo's was low and deep, treacle syrup. 'It's mainly to do with the manufacture and export of technological equipment and machine tools for agricultural applications.'

'What kind of agricultural applications?'

'Wheat development, soil testing, plant breeding, cloning, that kind of thing . . .'

The interrogator leaned forward, his hands gripping the edge of the table, his head pushed forward, a cat poised before its prey, waiting to pounce. 'You have infringed the COCOM rules,' he said.

'COCOM is an ass,' snapped Hugo. 'An instrument of Yankee paranoia that works against British trade interests. No sane British trader should have any truck with it.'

'The Co-ordinating Committee for Multilateral Export Control is a body of which this country is a member and we abide by its rules,' said the interrogator slowly, still straining forward. 'It has a duty to restrict the sale of advanced technology which could be used by the Soviet Union and its satellites for military purposes.'

'No one objects to the embargo of military and nuclear goods,' said Hugo. 'But the COCOM list of prohibited goods goes far beyond that and covers basic everyday technology like eight-bit personal computers. That's why it's a joke. A pernicious Yankee joke.' He looked warily at the interrogator. 'Do you know what an eight-bit computer is?'

'Never mind that,' shouted the interrogator. 'The fact is that you did not apply for the relevant licences.'

'Do you know how long it takes to apply for a licence? Ten months.'

'Did you apply for the relevant licences?'

'I've broken no British law.'

'Answer my question: did you or did you not apply for the relevant licences?'

'Is the use of American know-how reason enough to subject British trade to American export regulations? You tell me that.'

'I'll tell you this and you'd better listen and listen hard. You are suspected of having sold prohibited equipment to third countries and of having concealed these transactions by giving false information. You have sent cargoes under false labels. On other occasions, you have sent proscribed items under the right labels and with the appropriate licences to countries like Greece from where they were shipped on to the Soviet Union . . . Is that so or is it not?'

There was no response from Hugo. He was utterly calm, attentive.

The interrogator's face was flushed, contorted with angry indignation. He was out to break the man before him. His voice rose. 'It was then that the Soviets started to blackmail you. Either you did what they wanted, or they'd spill the beans. Was that so, or wasn't it?' As Hugo stared at him silently, he repeated the words, hammering the table with his fist. 'Was that so or wasn't it?' In the face of Hugo's continued silence, his voice soared to a scream. 'You suborned Maitland Ellis into working for the Soviets,' he shrieked. 'You were the sprat they used to catch a mackerel . . .'

The shrill, strident sound echoed in the room. The interrogator sat back.

'Prove it,' said Hugo calmly, his voice low, controlled. 'Prove it,' he said again. 'Prosecute me.'

And now the interrogator fell silent, staring at Hugo, his manufactured fury spent, discarded. After a while, he pressed a button on the tape recorder before him and they heard Hugo's voice say, 'May I speak to Mary Kaye?' A woman answered, 'There is no one of this name here.' And then Hugo's voice again. 'I am sorry: wrong number.'

'There is no Mary Kaye,' said the interrogator dismissively. 'But there is a woman who receives calls from people asking for Mary Kaye. That's her.'

They saw, projected on the screen, a shabbily dressed woman hurrying out of a block of flats. And then, in quick succession, a shot of the woman with a man who was said to be a known GRU illegal, and another of the illegal standing side by side with Hugo at a bar.

'Have you at any time clandestinely communicated official information to an unauthorized person?'

Hugo did not reply.

'Have you ever been approached by any person to pass information clandestinely?'

Hugo remained impassive.

For a while no one else spoke either. Hugo's composure was undented. The interrogator had shot his bolt. It seemed he'd lost out.

'We shall agree not to prosecute if you resign your seat and leave the country,' he said at last, almost rhetorically.

Hugo shrugged his shoulders and turned to look at Angela. She thought how strong he was. How sure. So

127

that when he spoke, she thought at first she had misheard him. As did the interrogator, for he asked Hugo to repeat his statement.

'So be it,' he repeated ironically. 'I accept the immunity deal lock, stock and barrel . . .'

'The first rule is know your enemy. And to do that, you must know who is the enemy. We wanted you present at Gray's interrogation so you could see his cloven foot for yourself . . .'

She had recognized him at once. He was the man in the pinstripe suit who had met David at Heathrow. He introduced himself as Neville Knight and said he was the case officer.

He had come to her after Hugo had left the house in South Audley Street. And now they were meeting in his office in Curzon Street – a narrow, coffin-shaped room overlooking the Mirabelle Hotel.

'There is something I must tell you,' she said. 'It was I who handed the notebook to him . . .'

Him. Not Hugo, not Gray or Mr Gray. Him. The man with the cloven foot. The man who betrayed his friend.

Knight smiled indulgently. 'No harm done. Quite the opposite in fact.' Underneath his affability – they were on the same side of the battle lines, weren't they? – was a cold, unwavering watchfulness.

'No harm done,' she repeated. 'I guess it is more or less what you and David had intended all along.' She tried her best to turn a grimace into a smile. 'The notebook as public exhibit number one.'

He did not respond.

'Intended to deceive the GRU that the duff information which David had fed them as your agent was in fact genuine.' She looked out of the window. 'Well, the message has got through to the Russians and you've been spared the embarrassment of a public trial. No harm done, as you say.'

Knight regarded her coldly. 'You feel let down and I don't blame you. But your husband had reasons for using the notebook as he did. He wanted to show the public that he had betrayed you too. He hoped that it would win you at least some sympathy as the wronged wife. Rightly or wrongly, Maitland Ellis thought that your marriage had died long ago and he never imagined that you'd want to stand up for him . . .'

'You make it sound as though he'd planned to kill himself.'

Knight looked at her with detached curiosity, like a chemist investigating the properties of an unknown substance. 'The plan was that he should be arrested and prosecuted . . .' He trailed off. 'However, that need not concern you. What matters is that you're now safe from the GRU.' She must have looked sceptical for he sounded faintly unnerved as he went on. 'Well of course you are. Gray is hardly likely to come clean with them, is he?'

'Why not?'

He laughed at her naïvety. 'Good heavens – It would mean putting his head on the block.'

She felt her face crumple up like a child about to burst into tears. Head bent, she started crying, and the more she wept, the more it seemed like a demeaning admission of weakness.

Her tears embarrassed Knight. 'There is no doubt at all of Gray's guilt, surely you must see that?' he said gravely. 'I was eavesdropping on the interrogation and must admit to some doubts of my own when I heard him challenge us to prosecute. But then he blew it. Agreeing to resign his

129

seat was a clear admission of guilt. Why else would he have given in?'

Why else? Because he was prepared to gamble his career and reputation as the price of her life? It didn't make sense. To protect David? But that too didn't make sense: David was dead, beyond protection. She felt she was beginning to understand that in the game of espionage, sentiment and compassion were trifles, irrelevant weaknesses. To give them weight was to misunderstand the rules of the game. He was probably right, she thought, as she gazed at Knight. There was only one possible reason why Hugo should have been prepared to give up his seat. And that reason was that he was guilty.

'And all this was quite unnecessary really,' said Knight. 'We would never have prosecuted him. It was the quid pro quo Maitland Ellis extracted from us before he agreed to name Gray.' He paused. 'I said you were safe from the KGB. You may not be safe from Gray.' He handed her a note with a phone number. 'Remember he is the enemy and stay on your guard. Let me know at once if he ever tries to contact you.'

'You're surely not suggesting that I am at risk from Hugo?' She laughed. The idea was preposterous. 'What possible threat could I be to him?'

He was looking at her legs. She was wearing green tights and leather pumps with a multi-coloured ethnic skirt, a T-shirt and a wide belt. She could tell he didn't approve of the way she dressed. Frivolous, he seemed to think. Unsuitable. He looked at her hair. Dyed. Red. He saw her as the kind of woman who would be taken in by Hugo's charm. A foolish woman out of her depth. 'Put yourself in his shoes,' he said calmly. 'He can rely on our silence since we've granted him immunity.' He smiled. 'But can he rely on your discretion?' He paused. 'Do you

130

realize that you are the only layperson who knows of his guilt . . .'

'Guilt . . .' she echoed. The word was heavy with moral censure. What was that passage in *1984* about a five-finger exercise? she asked herself. She did not know what Knight read in her response which caused him to say, 'You must understand that a spy is a person who operates at two levels. He may be a perfect friend or lover at one level, and a cold, ruthless killer at another.'

She nodded. It was no good, she thought. She and Neville Knight might be on the same side of the barricades but for all the empathy between them they might as well be on different planets.

She got up and held out her hand to take her leave. She was anxious to be gone. His handshake was like a vice.

20

Towards the end of May, just before the inquest into David's death was concluded, rumours started appearing in the British press that Poliakin, the man who had allegedly uncovered David as a spy, was himself becoming discredited and was now suspected of being a KGB plant. Like wildfire the rumours spread to the USA, and the *New York Times* reported that the CIA now believed that Poliakin's early leads which had helped to establish his credibility were in fact discards – agents the KGB had been prepared to sacrifice because they'd outlived their usefulness. Poliakin's real role, it was suggested, had been to sow discord between intelligence services in Europe and America by muddying the waters.

At about that time, during the Whitsun recess, Hugo Gray announced that he was applying for the Chiltern Hundreds and giving up his Parliamentary seat to return to journalism. He was quoted as saying he'd been offered a job as a foreign correspondent in Vienna and hoped to devote more time to writing about East-West affairs. Angela heard the news on the radio of her hired car as she was driving herself to the inquest, amidst fields of saffron-coloured rape seed.

The inquest heard evidence from the accident investigators who went over the events that led to the crash. The pilot had radioed air traffic control when he was over Carmarthen in Dyfed, and that was the last that was heard from him. The examination of the wreckage had subsequently established that the escape hatch had become loose, or had been deliberately loosened, during the flight, and it seemed that the accident happened because, instead of going up, the pilot suddenly dropped height on approaching the mountainside. It was this that caused the plane to crash into the mountain, and it wasn't clear why the plane should have descended instead of ascended.

One possible theory was pilot error. Poor visibility, combined with the stress caused by the defective escape hatch, could have resulted in the pilot suddenly becoming disorientated. Another possibility was that the escape hatch could have been deliberately loosened as a result of direct action, in which case the hatch could have struck the airbrake just before the accident happened. However, this theory seemed implausible because it implied that someone else would have been on board, in addition to the pilot, and only one body was recovered. A third possibility was that the accident was deliberate, and that the pilot had intended to kill himself. But it was also possible that the accident was due to another cause, an unknown factor that would never be discovered.

The inquest returned an open verdict.

The Poliakin affair and the inquest revived the Press's interest in the Maitland Ellis case. At Alice's insistence David's funeral was public, and she organized it in such a way that it became a testimonial to the Maitland Ellis family. David was buried at Holly Place under the shadow of tall trees, close to a memorial to his father. The staff of the special school were all present. Many of David's former colleagues and friends also came. Rather more friends of Fanny's turned up, wearing CND badges. And they were all outnumbered by the Press.

Before the committal, the minister read out Psalm 103.8 and the words tore at Angela's heart. 'The days of man

133

are but as grass: he flourishes like a flower of the field; when the wind goes over it, it is gone: and its place will know it no more.'

She knew now that in spite of everything she had loved David, and she knew that love was ravaged by death, that life was ravaged by death, that the grave had no voice.

Where are you? she asked in her heart. Come back. Come back. Come back.

The photograph which appeared in the following day's papers showed Angela dry-eyed and straight-backed at the mouth of the grave, the other mourners some distance behind her. It was only when she looked more closely at these newspaper photographs of the mourners that she detected, half-hidden at the back of the crowd, the tall thin figure of Neville Knight. A small woman with glasses was with him, and Angela recognized Harriett Osborne, David's secretary at the DTI. She knew now that Harriett Osborne was a security woman. Her job as David's secretary had been no more than a cover for her intelligence activities. Harriett Osborne had been David's link with MI5.

I should have known, thought Angela, as she remembered the coolly correct woman who'd held forth to her about moral philosophy. And although she could no longer remember precisely what Harriett had said, Angela thought a little ironically that it boiled down to nothing more than a dressed-up version of the statement that the end justified the means.

PART THREE
The Lobster Pot

21

January 1985. Angela was crossing Parliament Hill Fields in the early morning on her way to school. The day seemed frozen. The ground, the grass, were stiff with hoar frost. Head bent, shoulders hunched, she was making her way to the top of the hill when she noticed the squirrel. It lay on its side, barely stirring and stared dully at her out of one small, tired eye. She bent over it and the squirrel bared its teeth, a terrified, sick animal making a pretence of baring its teeth. Best to leave it alone, she thought, and moved on. But she hadn't got very much further when she saw two or three crows swoop down on the squirrel, and she watched horrifiedly as they started pecking at it as if trying to pluck its eyes out. She ran back towards the wounded beast, shouting at the top of her voice, swinging her scarf at the birds to frighten them away until they flew away with angry squawks and croaks. She bent down to the wounded squirrel. It looked out at her from its bloodied eye. It was dying, she thought. And then she heard a flapping of wings behind her, and as she turned, she saw one of the birds above her, its wings outstretched, croaking furiously. She watched it, aghast at being attacked by a crow. She noticed the broad black wings, rounded at the tips. But this couldn't be a crow, surely, could it? It was too large and too fierce and too much like a bird of prey. Was it a raven, perhaps? The bird dived towards her, with wings now folded, and she instinctively shielded her eyes with her arm and started running backwards, seeking shelter. But there was nothing behind her, no hiding place. She ducked, and gestured and shouted at the bird to frighten it away, then she heard a muffled sound behind her. The bird flew away but it was another, smaller bird, a crow, that had been hit. She watched its broken flight to the nearest tree, an oak tree, where it briefly perched on a branch before falling to the ground.

A man wearing a nondescript coat and tweed deer-stalker hat was making his way towards her. The brim of his hat was turned down and covered his brow. 'Vicious creatures, crows,' he said.

She did not immediately recognize Neville Knight. 'I thought it was a raven,' she answered. They did not otherwise greet each other but stood together staring at the dying squirrel at their feet. Knight pointed a revolver at the squirrel and pressed the trigger. The revolver was fitted with a silencer and there was hardly any noise. She watched the squirrel's body bounce up and fall back. It was dead, its eye still open. The act was curiously incongruous, like breaking a butterfly on a wheel.

She must have looked shocked for he said, 'It's all right. All right to shoot them, I mean. They're not a protected species.'

She wondered why it was that she and Neville Knight were always at cross-purposes.

A crow had perched on the oak tree. It was joined by one, and then two, three, four crows, and what soon seemed like a whole flock of black crows materialized as if out of thin air. They congregated desolately on the skeleton of that one single tree.

'I suppose it isn't mere accident that brings you here?' she asked Neville Knight.

One of the crows flew down to the dead crow and then flew back to its perch.

'You remember Poliakin?' he asked.

Another crow flew down to the dead bird. It seemed like a ritual. A crow funeral. She remembered that Poliakin was the KGB informer who'd gained the ear of the CIA but whom MI5 distrusted. They suspected him of being a plant because they knew that David, whom Poliakin had named, was in fact a double agent working for them.

'The CIA blew the gaff on MI5 by leaking Poliakin's allegations, that's what happened, wasn't it?' She thought it was hardly surprising that MI5 and the CIA did not trust each other, since no one trusted anyone in espionage.

'Let's just say that we work closer together these days,' said Knight. 'Anyhow, the point is that we decided to bring Poliakin to this country for a debriefing session, but he's given us the slip. We believe he is after you.'

'Me? Why me?' she asked. She was staring at the crows and found it hard to concentrate on what he was saying. Poliakin. 'What could he possibly want from me?'

'He maintains that he was discredited over the Maitland Ellis episode and says that your husband was a Soviet agent long before the Falklands War . . .'

'You mean before Hugo got him to spy for the Russians?' The croaking of the crows grew louder and angrier.

'That is his allegation. Needless to say, we do not attach much credence to it. But we consider that it would be most unwise for you to talk to Poliakin.'

'Why?' she asked. He spoke very formally but his words were all but drowned in the angry cries of the crows. She shivered as she looked at the black birds against the white, winter sky. They seemed like an omen of death.

'Because we fear that he might feed you a barium meal.'

She looked at him uncomprehendingly.

'Get you to say what he wants you to say to prove his allegations . . .' he added a trifle impatiently.

The birds on the oak tree were now silent. The crow funeral was over. They flew away, one by one, in different directions, disappearing as suddenly as they had appeared.

'You don't trust me much, do you?' she asked. Labelled in his mind as a slow learner.

He didn't reply.

They walked in silence until they reached the top of the hill. London lay at their feet in the valley below. Unremitting grey stone. Her head was still full of the black birds. Crows. Crow. *Corbeau. Corvo. Cuervo.* She shivered. Whose death did they presage? she wondered superstitiously. Who was to be the next victim?

'We suspect that Poliakin is in London. We would like you to go away until we've had a chance to catch up with him.'

She shook her head. She wished he would disappear like the black birds and vanish. 'I can't take time off,' she said calmly. 'I'm a teacher. I have a duty to my pupils . . .'

'There is no duty higher than duty to the State,' he said. He looked towards Westminster. 'Did you know that this hill was once known as Traitors' Hill in memory of Guy Fawkes? He and his men started off from here when they set out to blow up the Houses of Parliament . . .' He paused 'I wouldn't be asking you to leave London unless it was necessary. As it is, I can only appeal to your conscience.' He raised his deerstalker's hat in a curiously old-fashioned gesture and, without another word, left her, turning north towards Highgate. She watched his retreating figure for a while. A man who was not accustomed to shaking hands and whose handshake was like a vice. And then she made her way to Belsize Park and the school.

Crow. *Corbeau. Corvo. Cuervo.* Someone was done for, she thought. Someone was done for. But who?

22

The more Alice stoked the fire, the more smoke and the less fire there was. It was a Sunday. The central heating boiler had broken down and, with no prospect of early repairs, they'd had no alternative but to try to light a coal fire. Thin flames lapped the lumps of coal, casting light but no warmth.

'When was the chimney last swept?' asked Angela.

'Heaven knows,' said Alice. 'Hugo normally saw to things like that.' Still stoking the fire, she turned round and shot Angela a reproachful look. 'Amazing how much I relied on him. Hugo, I mean . . .' Meaning, thought Angela, Hugo, not David, or David's wife or David's children. Hugo, Alice's favourite.

Alice stood up, dusty and dishevelled. 'I give up,' she said, and put on a coat, then wrapped a blanket around it. She handed another blanket to Angela and they sat huddled up on each side of the non-existent fire.

'He helped decorate this room,' said Alice in the dark. Hugo, the absent Hugo. 'And the rest of the cottage too, for that matter.'

She mourned Hugo's absence as she had never mourned David's death, thought Angela. Because it was Hugo, not David, whom she'd loved.

'And all the while,' Alice went on, 'his own house was getting shabbier and shabbier. I had no idea. Did you?'

Angela shook her head. A sullen resentment filled her as she thought of David, who had sacrificed his life for Hugo.

'Why me?' asked Alice querulously. 'Why should Hugo ask an old woman like me to settle his affairs when he could turn to someone like you instead?' And as Angela still said nothing, 'When did you last see him?' she demanded.

'I honestly don't remember.' Angela was never much good at lying. The deception didn't seem worth the candle, somehow. 'Here, was it, a year ago now?'

Alice switched on a table lamp and looked at Angela with pursed lips, her small chin set in disapproving scepticism. If she had her hair tied in a bun at the back of her head she'd look like Queen Victoria, thought Angela. Small. Plump. Imperious. And very determined.

'When he attended the last meeting of Governors here at the school, he seemed like a stranger. A hostile stranger. Yet I had done nothing to betray his trust. But someone else had. One of us. And he would not tell me who. And nor would he tell me why he'd resigned his seat in Parliament . . .'

'He's still Chairman of the school Governors then?'

'And why should he not be?' challenged Alice. But Angela did not rise to the bait. 'Who else is there to be Chairman of Governors? You perhaps? Or Fanny? Me? Let's face it, without Hugo the school would go bankrupt and close down.' She waited for a retort that did not come. 'He's trying, even now, to help us. There's some talk of a legacy from a Canadian benefactor who had a grandchild at the school years ago, and Hugo is pursuing the matter from Vienna . . .' She got up and turned her back to the fireplace, facing Angela. 'But that's not the point, is it, Angela? The point is, why on earth should he have resigned his Parliamentary seat? I don't know why. But someone must know. You. You must surely know or suspect something . . .'

143

Angela shook her head.

'I don't believe you,' said Alice. 'Just as I don't believe you when you tell me you've come down here to recharge your batteries . . .'

'Why . . . Why don't you believe me?' Really, she thought, she didn't much care whether Alice believed her or not.

'Because you tell me that I'm not to say that you were feeling tired, if anyone asks. And that if anyone should ask, I am to tell them that I was ill and asked you to come.' She swept her hands through her hair in frenzied exasperation. 'I'm as fit as a fiddle, as well you know . . .'

'There was something else we needed to discuss,' said Angela. 'David's memorial stone. Shouldn't we decide what it should say?'

Alice shrugged. 'What they all say – "In memory of a loving and devoted husband and father". What else?'

You should care, thought Angela. You should have cared for David. But then, had she herself cared? Had she mourned him? The clock had never stopped after his death and now the days of his life were but as withered grass. They knew him no more.

Alice got up and started pacing up and down the room in an effort to keep warm. 'And then,' she said, as if speaking to herself, 'and then there's this poor sod who's on the run and of course, if I were to ask you, you'd tell me that you know nothing about that either, and it's nothing to do with your being here . . .'

Somehow, the Press had got wind of Poliakin's visit to Britain and his disappearance, and they'd set themselves on his trail, not knowing what he looked like, what name he used, or whether or not he was travelling alone. They'd also reported that Angela had left London for an unknown destination.

'What's his name?' demanded Alice.

'Poliakin?' asked Angela. 'Poliakin,' she repeated. How familiar that name had become to her. Poliakin. She felt she knew him. Emotional, obstinate, self-important, something of an egomaniac. And doomed. Like David had been doomed.

Alice took a slip of paper out of her coat pocket which she handed to Angela. 'I came across this while I was clearing Hugo's house.'

It was a note in Angela's handwriting, and as she looked at it she wondered at the unformed scrawly letters, so unlike Alice's beautiful, clear script. The note was undated but she guessed she'd written it at the time Hugo had stayed with them in Highgate. He was still a journalist then and had not yet entered Parliament.

'I'm like a plant that's pot-bound,' says Hugo. 'The pot is too small and I'm beginning to wither. But you,' he tells David, 'you're in the wrong soil. Whilst Angela is a cactus. Able to survive in any soil.' They smile at me, David and Hugo, Hugo and David, and for once I do not feel excluded. I belong.

And may we never come to hate one another.

Silently, Angela handed the note back to Alice who crumpled it into a ball and tossed it in the cold grate.

'You know something and will not tell me,' she said bitterly. 'And if there's anything I hate it's being deceived by those I trust. Really, I'd much rather you didn't come here any more if you're not going to be honest with me, Angela.'

Angela felt tears well up in her eyes. Tears of resentment, not guilt. Tears for David, the unbeloved. Not for Hugo. Or herself. Or even Alice.

* * *

The temperature dropped below freezing point during the night and the two women sat in their armchairs, frozen in sleepless isolation. When Angela left the cottage at dawn, Alice had at last fallen asleep and she did not wake her up. She left Holly Place as if for the last time.

A blanket of freezing fog lay over the village in the valley. As she drove past the old post office she saw a car ahead of her blocking the road. She stopped and got out. The car was empty but the key was nowhere. She looked around and noticed something dangling from a tree on the village green. A dummy, she thought. She was drawn towards it and as she walked towards it the grass under her feet was like shards of glass. The body was covered in ice crystals. The shoes were real enough – heavy leather brogues – and the trousers too – tweeds with old-fashioned turn-ups. She stumbled against something in the fog, a small wooden stool. She reached out for something to cling to in an effort not to lose her balance, and grasped the dummy's trousers, not the dummy itself. But it was no dummy. It was a corpse, heavy with rigor mortis. She lifted her hands and something fell out, something he'd hidden inside the turn-ups of his trousers. It was a slip of paper, folded tight like a hand-rolled cigarette. She opened it and saw her name and the address of Holly Place written out in black ink in a slanted, foreign script.

They got you, she thought as she looked at the body of Poliakin hanging in an English field that would be forever Soviet. She looked at his face through the freezing fog. The eyes, still open, stared blindly, vitreous, vacuous, dead. The skin of his face clung, wax-like, to the skull. The hair was scraped back, flat, grey. And the mouth, bloodless, lifeless, was wide open in a rictus of pain.

The mortal remains of a living presence. A man. Some

mother's son. Some daughter's father. She looked at his dead eyes and in her mind she saw the eye of the dying squirrel. Crow. *Corbeau. Cuervo. Corvo.* She felt implicated. Guilty of this man's death.

She stared at his mouth. Her own mouth opened as if to utter a scream. She wanted to shout something. A name. Some name. Somebody's name. But no name came to mind and the scream stuck in her throat.

23

Admittedly, it had been her own decision. Given the choice of a solid, traditional secondary school of the kind her own children had attended, and this particular one in a tough area of North London, she'd opted for the latter. Housed in a forbidding Victorian building with narrow corridors and peeling paint, it had the advantage of being led by an inspirational Head determined to turn the school around. It was the kind of challenge that had drawn Angela, but now, in her second term at the school, she'd got tired of playing Pollyanna to a bunch of punks.

That morning she walked into the noisy classroom and, as always, the din did not abate. These tough, streetwise kids brought up in mean estates on mean streets surrounded by North London arty poshness didn't go in for namby-pamby stuff like standing up for the teacher or even saying hello. They went on chatting amongst themselves – it was for the teacher to teach and for them to resist being taught, wasn't it? And for once she neither wheedled nor cajoled, but just ignored them. Walked in, turned her back on them, wiped out the graffiti on the blackboard, took a piece of chalk – lucky to find some – and started writing.

''Ere Miss, you ain't said *bonjour* this morning,' said one bright spark.

She ignored that, too, and went on writing in large block capitals that filled half the board. '*LOTERIE* = RAFFLE'. Quietly, slowly, she put the chalk back, wiped her hands, and then deliberately sat on the desk, crossing her legs before her. From that vantage point she could see them all and they had to look up to her.

'You know what a raffle is in French, don't you, 4B? I've written the word on the board. *Une loterie.*' She had tried in the past to use only French in speaking to them. The kind of French they might find relevant. About travel, for instance. Or booking a hotel. Holidays. Pop. Football. All to no effect. She might as well have been talking to herself for all the contact she'd managed to establish with them. But they were listening now, watchfully attentive, and, at any other time, holding them in the palm of her hand would have been heady exhilaration.

Any other time but now.

'I've won first prize at a raffle organized for the local hospital. *Le premier prix.* And do you know what it is I've won?' She paused. 'A trip to Quebec for the winter carnival next month. No less.'

She wrote it on the board: *VACANCES AU CANADA*.

They oohed and aahed and corred and blimeyed and said it weren't half bad, and some people had all the luck, and why was she so miserable about it then, didn't she know a good thing when she saw one?

She had a captive audience. Perhaps, she thought inconsequentially, perhaps there was something to be said for old-fashioned chalk and talk as a means of engaging a class's interest.

'But there's a mystery attached to this prize,' she said. 'Can anyone guess what it is?'

White faces, black faces, boys' faces, girls' faces, equally hostile now. But curious. Suspicious. And involved. They'd seen her picture in the papers. They knew it was she who'd found Poliakin's body hanging from a tree.

A week after Poliakin's death a coroner had recorded a

149

verdict of suicide. A pathologist had told the inquest that Poliakin had been asphyxiated due to hanging and that there was no evidence to suggest involvement by any other person. His findings were supported by a second pathologist. And although some intelligence specialists had claimed that the hanging had the hallmarks of a KGB killing, the police had found no evidence to support that claim. But the suspicion lingered that Poliakin had been assassinated.

The kids in 4B were not alone in suspecting that Angela was the widow of a traitor. They knew, these kids, that there was nothing worse than a traitor – not burglars, thieves, rapists or abusers. For traitors let the country down. They betrayed the rest of us to the enemy.

Angela's voice rose. 'I never entered for that raffle,' she said. 'Someone else did so in my name.' She looked at them, her gaze going from one to another. One of these little gits had played a trick on her. Who? 'I'm waiting for someone to tell me who bought a ticket in my name.'

A hand shot up. Not you, Martin, she thought. My one good pupil.

'I know who done it, Miss . . .' he said. 'It's them blighters, MI5. They're all the same, cops. They play dirty . . .'

Someone who was a policeman's cousin thumped Martin and called him a nerd. Martin was slight, sickly and short-sighted. The policeman's cousin was a thirteen-stone girl bully. Others who felt they had an interest in the matter of law and order joined in too, and the fight developed into a scrum with arms and legs hitting out in all directions. Martin emerged from the tussle like a drowning man gulping for air, his glasses broken, his nose bleeding, and then went down again shouting for help.

Angela was voiceless. She could neither shout nor scream. She took off her shoes and dived into the mêlée, dishing out wallops left and right, and pulling the most aggressive back by their hair. One of them lashed out and punched her in the face. The other kids shouted that he'd bashed the teacher and in the sudden silence Angela faced her assailant. He wore a ring on every finger. It wasn't clear for a moment whether he would hit Angela or back down. Angela took no chances and slapped him first. 'Stop this racket at once and go back to your places.'

To her surprise, they did as she said, staring at her with grins on their faces.

''Ere, Miss,' said the class clown. 'What's French for a shiner then?'

'Being right is not enough. Cassandra was right and see where it got her,' said Shirley, the Head. 'There's no excuse for unprofessional conduct. Even if one of your pupils had played a trick on you – which I doubt, incidentally, since these kids have better things to do with their money than squander it on raffle tickets – it is fatal to provoke confrontations in the classroom. The art of good classroom management is dead simple. Avoid confrontations. Period.'

Shirley was a good sort, an unwoolly socialist who could be ruthless when necessary and was particularly good at bringing the best out of unpromising people and situations. But now she was seething. 'In any school other than this you'd have parents up in arms alleging you'd assaulted their children, and your head would be on the block . . .'

Angela had felt more assaulted than assaulting. She mustered as much dignity as she could behind the dark glasses hiding her black eye and opened her mouth to

151

speak, and then shut it again. She had difficulty finding her voice these days. Or knowing what to say.

'Listen, Angela,' said Shirley, not unkindly. 'You're responsible for the care and safety of your pupils, and if you want their respect you should show some respect for them too.' She saw Angela's scepticism. 'Well, yes, I would say that, wouldn't I? More to the point – aren't you being a bit paranoid?'

'Am I? But if they didn't do it, who did? Somebody bought fifty quids' worth of tickets in my name. Why?'

'Does it matter? You won a holiday or someone won it for you. What difference does it make? Take it. Let your hair down. Enjoy yourself. You need a break and the kids need cooling off. It could do the school a lot of good . . .'

Angela felt like a puppet made to dangle on a string by an unseen puppet master. 'Fine,' she said. 'Fine.' She knew from experience that there was no point arguing with Shirley once she'd made up her mind.

24

Angela left for Canada in a state of utter disorganization, phoning her neighbours from the airport to ask them to turn off the gas and electricity. She slept for most of the journey, and when she arrived in Montreal the Mirabel Airport seemed oddly vast and silent after the hustle and bustle of Heathrow. She wandered around the airport's lounges and walkways, surprised at the vast empty spaces around her. She'd expected to be met on arrival, but there was no one waiting for her, no messages, and no one turned up. Over a cup of coffee at a cafeteria she took a hard look at the two-page itinerary she'd received in London a week before and hadn't yet properly read. There were details of her programme (a week in Quebec City for the winter carnival and in between a few days in Montreal), train times to and from Quebec, hotels where accommodation had been booked for her, as well as hints about restaurants and things to see and do during her visit. But that was all. There were no names and no point of contact in Canada. She was on her own.

They – whoever had organized her trip – had carefully picked the hotel they booked her into at Montreal. It was the top part of a futuristic, multi-level concrete and glass complex where the lower levels consisted of terraces and balconies built around a sunken plaza with waterfalls, hanging plants, trees and gardens. Here were shops, boutiques, restaurants and coffee bars. In the hotel itself, her room was much like any room at a luxury hotel in Europe – *en suite* bathroom, TV set, thick carpeting, soft lighting, neutral colours, discreet pictures on the walls. But it was bigger and there was also a surprisingly large unframed mirror in the middle of one wall, facing an intercommunicating door to a neighbouring room.

Angela looked around her. She felt as if the room had been taken over and turned into a stage set. She could not understand why she felt overlooked. She peered into the mirror and saw nothing but her reflection peering at herself. A game of mirrors. She went to the window and looked out. It was snowing, and the snow had piled up on the rooftops, hanging over the edges in long, spear-like icicles.

It was bitterly cold outside, several degrees below freezing point. She took refuge at first in the underground city, the subterranean network housing shops, restaurants, discos, bars, banks and cinemas that formed an alternative city insulated from the weather outside. But even in this warm honeycomb she could not shake off the feeling of being watched – something she brushed off as a traveller's normal feeling of estrangement in a new world.

Above ground the city's higgledy-piggledy assembly of the sacred and the profane, the new and the old, big business and folk, sport and the arts, Nouvelle France and cosmopolitan metropolis formed so many vignettes that dazzled but did not cohere. Downtown. The old city. Venerable cathedrals. Big-money banking centres. Expo' 67. The Olympic Park. Cobbled streets. Luxury stores. Small bookshops. Chinatown. French, Greek, Italian, Polish and Japanese restaurants. She saw these things and they were pictures of the mind. One day she would forget them. Unlike the old woman kneeling in the crypt of St Joseph's Oratory before the rows of crutches left behind by miraculously cured pilgrims, her arms wide open in supplication. That picture became imprinted in her heart

154

and she would remember it. She would remember wishing at that moment that she too could pray. For David perhaps. For David whom she had not mourned and had never really understood. She lit a candle and the flickering flame rose and trembled in the cold morning air.

She returned to the hotel and went to her room to pack for her journey to Quebec the next day. It was noon. The man next door – she assumed it was a man – had already left. She had not seen him but they kept each other awake. Where she was early to rise and early to bed, he did not surface before noon or turn in before midnight.

Automatically, she turned the handle of the intercommunicating door to check that it was locked. It was open. She looked in. The room next door was the mirror image of her own. She walked in. It was so scrupulously tidy, there was hardly any sign of a presence there. She opened the door of the fitted cupboards and saw a suitcase placed on top of the row of drawers. It was locked. A drawer underneath was slightly ajar. Inside it was a pair of pyjamas untidily crumpled up in a small heap. He must have thrust them away and then forgotten to pack them with the rest of his things. Or perhaps he was surprised by someone coming in. They were plain cotton pyjamas with a thick blue stripe. She patted them and felt something hard.

A small, pistol-like crossbow was hidden under the pyjamas. It held a bolt of about six inches with a black arrowhead and a sharp, steel-tipped end. Was this a weapon, a sports implement or a toy? Angela could not tell.

Back in her room, she phoned the reception desk and asked them to bring a key to lock the intercommunicating door. She thought no more of the crossbow and slept soundly that night before leaving the hotel the next morning at the start of her journey to Quebec City and the winter carnival.

25

The lounge below deck was packed with boisterous revellers. The weather was icy cold and the ferry sliced through island-like ice floes as it sailed across the St Lawrence from Levis to Quebec. Halfway through the crossing, Angela made her way to the deck above, and as she looked up through the falling snow she caught her breath, spellbound at the vision of a French château rising sharply from the cliff face, its spires, turrets and towers reaching up to the skies.

It shouldn't be there, she thought. Gazing at the fairy-tale apparition on top of the cliff, she struggled to recall dates, centuries, historical events. It can't be, she thought again, smiling as she wiped the snowflakes from her face. Even if this were a late-vintage château built in the Renaissance, Quebec would only just have been discovered then, and no one could have dreamt of building a château in the middle of a wilderness.

The improbable castle cocking a snook at history delighted her, and the feeling of enchantment and anachronism persisted after the boat landed in Quebec.

She travelled by taxi up to the gates of the old city and then walked through the arched Gate of St Louis with its Gothic turrets and crenellated gun-ports. It had stopped snowing now and as she walked past the lovely Norman houses on the Rue St Louis that had been turned into restaurants, rooming houses and boutiques, a festive crowd spilled out of the old buildings onto the street. Walking through the crowd, her suitcase in one hand, she felt like a stranger stepping into a *fête étrange*, a lost domain, and she was filled with a yearning for joy.

They'd booked her in at a Nouvelle France *auberge* which was on the route of the midnight carnival parade. Her room – one of three on the top floor – had a heavy, old-fashioned wardrobe, starched bed linen smelling of lavender, and an atmosphere of provincial France. There was no separate bathroom, merely a hand-basin and shower cubicle. But here was the same large, unframed mirror as in the hotel in Montreal and, as in Montreal, an intercommunicating door to the next room.

She opened it, a mirrored box opening onto another box with a similar mirror on a parallel wall.

A man stood with his back to her, facing the mirror, and their eyes met in the glass. He wore a black ski suit and a Pierrot mask on his face. The face was painted white. The eyes were brown. They were rimmed with black and two painted tears fell out of one eye. The red mouth, like a clown's, was turned down at the corners.

He stared at her in obvious alarm and drew back, still gazing at her reflection in the glass, as if about to spring forward.

'It's all right,' she said quickly. 'I didn't mean to startle you. I have the room next door . . .'

The words did not seem to register with him. Perhaps, she thought, he did not understand English. '*Excusez-moi*,' she said. '*Je ne voulais pas vous effrayer . . .*'

He nodded and smiled, seemingly reassured. His smile radiated a fugitive gentleness that held her in thrall. She did not know how long they stood staring at each other thus in the glass. She moved towards him and the smile froze on the masked face, which became contorted with rage. He turned and caught her by the arm, pushing and

158

bundling her back into her own room, then he slammed the door shut between them.

She leaned against that closed door and shuddered, unnerved that he should have been so different from the person she had briefly imagined. There was a ruthlessness in him, a barely contained violence that was a little like madness.

She tried to put the episode out of her mind and started unpacking her things, but the image of the Pierrot's painted tears on his angry face preyed on her.

In spite of the icy cold, Quebec turned into a massive funfair for the winter carnival with dancing in the streets, an ice palace, ice sculptures, canoe races across the St Lawrence, motorcycle races on ice, winter sports, carnival parades, a carnival queen, bonfires, fireworks. The revellers kept warm and merry on Caribou, a cocktail made of spirits and sweet red wine, and the carnival proceeded under the presiding spirit of Bonhomme Carnaval, a huge snowman wearing a French revolutionary cap and Indian herringbone sash.

Angela was alone in the midst of that explosion of joy, and much as she wanted to join in the merrymaking, something kept her apart and separate. She was a stranger, an outsider, she did not belong.

She did not immediately feel alarmed when the phone calls started. They were anonymous. When she answered, there was only silence. But there, at the other end, was someone. Perhaps the Pierrot. It was a kind of contact.

To start with, she too was silent. Then one evening, emboldened by Caribou, she started talking to him, or perhaps to herself. 'I love this place,' she said, 'and yet nothing is quite what it seems. Not the Gate of St Louis, which has been relocated and rebuilt, and not the Château

159

Frontenac that's no castle but a hotel. And you, you're not what you seem, are you? Who are you behind your mask? Are you hiding?'

'Have you seen the inscription over the old post office?' she asked when he phoned again. 'It's about the dog that bides his time. He will bite the biter – "A time will come when I shall bite he who bit me." Are you the biter or the bit?'

'Are you stalking me?' she asked when the phone rang the next day. 'Are you stalking me?'

He phoned again later the same day. 'Who are you?' she asked. 'Is that you, Hugo?'

And then she heard her voice being played back to her over the phone. 'A time will come when I shall bite he who bit me.'

She put the receiver down, her hand shaking, suddenly terrified.

26

Leaning over the rail on the edge of Dufferin Terrace, she was watching a canoe race on the partly frozen St Lawrence. The five men in each craft partly canoed, partly pushed their canoe forward over the ice floes. Angela looked around her. Behind, to the south, the Promenade des Gouverneurs led to the citadel and the Plains of Abraham, where two centuries before the French and English had massacred one another for the conquest of Quebec. Beyond, to the north, the heights of Dufferin Terrace and the wide ramparts bristling with cannons towered above the narrow streets and old houses of the lower town at the foot of the steep cliff. The signs of strife, battle and conflict were everywhere in this city, unnervingly neutralized into parks and tourist attractions.

A colourful crowd was watching the canoe race on the river. She scanned the faces around her. There was no one here she knew, but then how could she expect to know what the Pierrot looked like without his mask? He might be any man in this crowd. He might be the man next to her and she wouldn't know. Unless the man in the mask was Hugo.

She had tried to get in touch with Neville Knight in London but when she phoned his number the person who answered told her he was on leave and would not be back for another fortnight. She asked to speak to Harriett Osborne but was told there was no one of that name there.

Restless, but determined not to return to the hotel, she

decided to visit the lower town after the canoe race was over. Avoiding the Breakneck Steps, she boarded the funiculaire, a small, cogwheel-operated cable car, to travel down to the bottom of the cliff. A few minutes after it started, the cable car juddered and jerked to a standstill, and as Angela looked nervously back to Dufferin Terrace she thought she saw the tall figure of a man in black. But it was a false alarm. The cable car soon resumed its journey and safely reached the terminus in the lower town.

It was bitterly cold. Freezing winds from the river swept across the narrow streets of brick and stone old houses with their steeply sloping roofs and tall chimneys. The whole area was being restored to its seventeenth- and eighteenth-century appearance and some of the restored houses had been turned into workshops and craft shops, restaurants and boutiques.

And then down a narrow, dark alley buried in snow, she noticed a near-derelict house awaiting restoration. There was a danger sign outside the house warning passers-by to keep away, but the door was wide open and flapping in the wind. It seemed to have been forced open. As she peered inside, Angela saw a narrow corridor leading to an inner door. Something, a doll perhaps, was leaning against that door. She hesitated. The alley itself was deserted but there were comings and goings round the corner, people were about. She stepped into the narrow corridor, irresistibly drawn by the mysterious doll.

The doll was a Pierrot, with a white face and two painted tears falling out of one eye.

Clutching the doll, she tried to open the inner door to the house. It was locked but it had a kind of glass window that would have been covered with a lace curtain in the past and was now bare. Inside was a low-ceilinged parlour and a staircase to the upper floor. The back windows were boarded up. There was an indefinable sense of menace. It was then that she heard a noise above her head as if someone were lurking on the floor above. She ran out of the house, still clutching the doll.

Something or someone hit her hard in the chest, leaving her breathless and confused. She felt herself half-carried half-dragged forward by heaving bodies clad in black, and she was too dazed to protest or struggle. They all collapsed like a pack of cards when a great boulder came crashing down in the snow, just missing them.

Angela looked up and saw the man in the Pierrot mask at the window of the derelict house. He drew back and moments later they heard the sound of a window being opened at the back and a muffled thud. They assumed the man had jumped out from a back window on the first floor.

Angela stood up and looked down at the rock-like boulder. He'd meant to kill her.

'*Vous l'avez échappé belle.*' The woman who spoke wore a starched white coif and wimple round her face and a black veil and robe. Angela recognized the habit of the sisters of the Good Shepherd. The nun spoke in a nasal Québecois which Angela did not at first understand.

'Yes, it was a close shave, wasn't it?' said another in a clipped English accent. She wore aviator-type glasses with tinted lenses.

'What was he like?' asked Angela rhetorically.

'*Il avait l'air anglais,*' said another nun. There were five or six of them and they stood together, shoulder to shoulder.

'This is a Québecois expression which loosely translated means that he looked decidedly odd . . .' And that time the accent was American and the voice a man's. The nun,

163

for it was a nun speaking, raised a hand to her face as if to shield it.

Angela noticed that there were hairs on the back of that hand. She looked from one to the other of that strange, multi-national group. Were they genuine nuns or revellers dressed up as nuns? And then, like one person, the nuns took to their heels and started to run.

'You saved my life,' Angela shouted after them, but they did not turn back, and she stood watching them as they sped away in their black robes like a single flock. And then they were gone. She was alone again.

The Pierrot doll lay at her feet. She bent down to pick it up, tears streaming down her face. She felt helpless, a defenceless woman trying to control the uncontrollable.

27

She had been unable to sleep and left the hotel at first light. For once Quebec was deserted. She stood at the last of the pavilion bandstands on Dufferin Terrace by the Plains of Abraham with the frozen river before her, the Appalachian foothills in the distance, and the rolling fields covered in snow behind her, and everything – the sky, the earth, the river – everything was winter whiteness in a world of immense solitude. She felt she had at last found the real Quebec. Kebec, the place where the river narrowed, timeless and peaceful.

The wooden circular pavilion with its delicate pointed roof and spire was covered in snow, and the wrought-iron posts stood out black against the white sky, whilst a row of tall lanterns lined Dufferin Terrace.

She knew he was there, knew it even before she turned round and saw him standing opposite her on the pavilion stage, wearing his Pierrot mask.

There should be music, she thought, and we might dance together to the music of time.

His hands were joined and he raised his arms towards her, pointing a pistol-like object which she knew to be the crossbow. He looked at her detachedly, unemotionally, as he coldly took aim, pointing the weapon at her head.

She was utterly unafraid and didn't much care whether she lived or died. 'I have always loved you,' she said, but it sounded trite. That wasn't what she meant to say. 'And now I have found you out,' she added.

She did not know why she said it but he shook his head

165

violently, and she could not understand why he should be so disturbed.

'I have found you out,' she said again, and sensed the struggle within him. 'I know you now,' she said, but did she? She saw him hesitate and then raise his arms almost imperceptibly, so that when he shot the dart it came whistling past just above her head and then fell in a wide arc down the cliffside towards the river. Gasping, she followed its trajectory with her eyes. When she turned round she saw him running in the snow across the Plains of Abraham.

28

That night she dreamt someone was making love to her. She knew it was a dream for there was no roughness in that lovemaking, just the caress of a lover's kiss, the touch of his skin, his limbs brushing hers. She smiled and in her dream he kissed the smile on her lips. She reached out to him, crying out. Make love to me. Please make love to me.

The sound of her own voice woke her up. She sat up in bed and saw him standing naked and unmasked in the doorway between their rooms, a light shining behind him. And for a moment neither of them spoke and she didn't know whether she was awake or still dreaming.

He walked in, a dark shadow, his naked body menacing. He came to her bed and, standing at her side, he seized her by the upper arm, pulling her up to her feet. His fingers pressed into her flesh, hurting her. She felt crushed by the force of his grip. She looked up at him, taken aback by his strength. There was a look in his eyes she had never seen before. It was pain, not anger.

'You know me then, Angela, do you?' he said in a hissed whisper. She could feel his breath on her face and turned away. 'You've found me out, have you?' He gripped her upper arms, bodily lifting her so that her face was against his.

'Let go,' she said angrily. 'Let go of me.'

He released her and as she fell he pulled her hair back so that her face was raised up to his and she was forced to look at him.

'Take a good look at me. You know me, do you? You know me?' he said, his face twisted, distorted. 'Well, let me tell you something. There is no one there. No one. I am no one . . .'

Her neck ached unbearably. 'Please let me go,' she pleaded. 'You'll break my neck.'

But he merely pulled tighter, forcing her head further back. 'I have been this indeterminate person who could be anything and everything – statesman and spy, husband and father, friend and foe. I could create and recreate myself into anything I pleased. Anything but a lover. Because I was no one and there was no one to love . . .' The words flowed, unstemmable. 'You thought you loved me,' he went on, 'but what you loved was an image. The image I created of myself. It was fake.' Relentlessly he pulled tighter and she cried out in pain. 'And yet you say you know me. It's a lie. You know me no better than anyone else, no better than Ivanov, Wright, the Osborne woman, or even Hugo, who all thought they knew me. They were fools. And Hugo was the biggest fool of all . . .'

And then at last he set her free. 'What are you saying?' she asked helplessly. 'What are you saying?' she repeated, rubbing her neck, not looking at him.

'I am saying that I want to live and damn the lot of them. They will not get me . . .' He cupped her jaw in his hands, and again raised her face to him. 'You know me then, do you?' he asked. 'You know me? Listen,' he said. 'Listen to me and try to understand. It all started when I was still at Eton. It was then that I was recruited to the Party. Later, at Cambridge, I joined the Russian Intelligence Service. I thought I did so because I hated class and privilege and wanted to work for the class struggle. In reality I thought I would be free as a spy. Free. A free man spying for equality and historical determinism. Can you understand that?'

She was struggling to understand. She nodded and he smiled, his hands still cupping her face. 'It was a sham,' he said. 'Trickery of another order. It wasn't long before I realized what a squalid business spying was. And by then my Plimsoll line of decency had become practically invisible. For a while I deceived myself into thinking that I could serve both sides and help build bridges between them. I told myself that what secrets I betrayed were small beer, matters of no importance that could not be prejudicial to the national interest . . .'

His hands slipped down her body, pushing the straps of her nightdress off her shoulders. 'But after Czechoslovakia I knew that I had no faith left in Communism, and I wanted out. I became a sleeper. I thought I was rid of them but I should have known that a spy can never be free. Black Panthers and Red Brigaders can turn pink, green or orange and no one bats an eyelid. But old Marxists like me only get stuck in a time warp and there's no way out of the lobster pot.'

And then she understood. 'You framed Hugo . . .' she said in a whisper.

He looked at her coldly. 'Yes,' he said calmly. 'I sold him down the river.'

She shook herself free and moved away. 'Why?' she demanded. 'Why? Did you hate him so much that you had to destroy him?'

He pulled her back to him. 'I had no choice,' he said. 'The GRU had me by the short and curlies. And since I could not tell MI5 that it was me they were blackmailing, I said it was Hugo.'

'And all the while, Hugo was innocent?'

He nodded. 'I smeared him,' he said. 'And they

believed me. Because I belonged, I fitted in, I was one of them, and Hugo wasn't.'

'He didn't betray you,' she said. 'He stood up for you.'

'He couldn't,' he said curtly. 'Couldn't betray me if he tried. He could never prove he was not guilty because you cannot prove the negative.' He looked away. 'And besides, he always had that one fatal weakness – goodness.' He placed his hands on her temples and pressed hard. 'Look at me. Take a good look. I am showing you everything that's rotten in me. Do you still think you know me?'

'What did you do?' she asked. 'What did you do as a double agent?'

He hesitated. 'MI5 used me to sow disinformation on NATO tactics and our defence technology. They staged my disappearance after the CBS leak because they could not risk a security trial . . .'

'You weren't in that plane then?'

'Only at first. And then I made an unscheduled stop at a pre-arranged spot and got out. A man from the SAS took my place and together we loaded a stiff on board. A corpse. The body that was found in the wreckage. The man whose identity I took over. The SAS man ejected just before the crash and made his escape under cover of darkness . . . It was a risky operation but it came off . . .'

He stopped abruptly, as if tiring of explanations. Impatiently, with both hands, he ripped the nightdress apart and tore it off her body. She stood naked before him. And before she could understand what was happening, he pushed her hard so that she fell back on the bed and he fell on top of her. She struggled against him but he was too strong for her. He pinned her down with his body, gripping her breasts and she felt his lips on her nipples, sucking, biting, kissing.

'No,' she cried. 'No. No. No . . .'

'I died when I was seven,' he said. 'My mother abandoned me because I was no good . . .' His hand moved down to her legs, parting them, reaching up between them. 'Do you hear?' he said. 'I died when I was seven and I have hidden ever since. I became no one . . .'

She could feel the urgency and desperation in him, but still she was pushing his hand away, his hand that was rough, not gentle, and tore at her flesh, hurting her.

'And then you turned up and I tried to kill you because I thought you were part of a plot to get me. But you told me you knew me, and I knew then that I wanted to recreate myself as myself, with you . . .'

There were no more guards, barbs or masks now, no secrets and no lies. The masquerade was over. What he wanted from her was the sense of his own identity, an unconditional acceptance of what he was, as a gift of love. Love, right or wrong. And something in her froze. It was too easy, she thought, looking at him, too easy to claim to be no one. He had been unscrupulous in his betrayal of country and friend, and he had been prepared to kill to save his skin. She felt herself physically recoiling from him, and he paused and moved back as if he could now see himself through her eyes. And then she saw the tears on his face glistening, and she sensed that he was trapped by immense and impersonal forces that threatened to crush him. She knew then that whatever he was, and whatever he'd done, she loved him.

She raised herself on the bed and wrapped her arms round his neck, her legs round his buttocks, pulling him down to her. 'Come to me, come to me, my love, come to me, now, now, now . . .'

He entered her, thrusting deep inside her, moaning and

171

straining. She wanted to touch him with every part of her, her hands, her breasts, her belly, her legs, her sex. She wanted him to fill her whole being.

And then he came inside her and screamed a name, his name, David.

Their happiness was fragile. A traitor is never an admissible person, he said. She held him – he was her husband, lover and child and he had suffered enough. She told him that the truth was always admissible, that he was only a boy when he'd made his commitment to Communism, that he had endured in the face of considerable odds, and that they would continue to endure. Together. They would find a place by a lake in the wilderness of the Canadian North where no one would find them and they would be safe and happy. And if it wasn't that year, it would be next year, or the year after, but it would happen some day.

He shook his head. 'You must face up to the fact that I have done great harm in my life,' he said. 'Less to England, my England, that is not an Old Etonian England, than to people, my people. The damage I have done Hugo cannot be undone.' He shrugged. 'But first things first. Tell me how you came to be here.' And as she shook her head, he insisted. 'Now,' he said. 'Now,' he repeated. 'Don't you see? It could be a matter of life and death. They could all be after me. The KGB. MI5. CIA. The bloody lot of them . . .'

'MI5?' she queried. 'Why MI5?'

'Because they will have realized by now that Poliakin told the truth and that I was a mole long before I became a double agent.'

She told him of the raffle. He asked whether she was present at the draw. Whether she knew that the winning

172

counterfoil was in her name. Whether she was asked for the ticket. Dully, numbly, she heard herself say that she had received the winning ticket by post, anonymously, the day she had been told she'd won the raffle.

Inexorably, a pattern began to unfold in her mind. She told him how she had discovered he was in the room next to her in Montreal. 'Didn't you know?' she asked gently, very gently, so as not to alarm him.

He shook his head. 'And you?' he asked, equally gently. 'Didn't you think that strange at the time?'

'I thought I was being stalked by Hugo . . .' she said. 'And then, when I got here, I realized without admitting it to myself that it was you . . .' She smiled, she tried to smile. 'I wasn't taken in by the brown lenses . . .'

'And the nuns,' he asked, 'what manner of fish were they?'

She told him what she could remember of them and he asked what the English nun was like.

'Young. Or youngish. And she wore glasses. Aviator-type glasses.'

'Like Harriett Osborne?' he queried.

She was unnerved. 'No – glasses with tinted lenses.' She watched with a feeling of doom as David prowled around the room, looking for clues, looking for bugs. 'Surely you don't think Harriett would be in Quebec dressed up as a fake nun?'

He laughed, almost gaily. 'She'd make a better leg person than that old stick Knight. And if the nuns are a mixed task force – MI5, CIA and the Canadian intelligence services – it would make sense to include in it someone who knows us both.'

Had they used her as a decoy to trap David?

'The mirror,' he said at last. He reached out for something on the dressing table, a jar of face cream, and thrust it with all his might against the glass. It shattered

173

loudly, shards of glass flying in all directions, revealing a hidden camera pointing at the room.

Swiftly, he pulled a wire at the back of the camera, disconnecting it. He turned to Angela. He was brisk and unafraid. 'The place is probably wired up for sound as well. They'll be here any minute now,' he said. There was a strange excitement in him. He seemed eager for action. For some kind of resolution.

She sat back on the bed, still naked. Softly, he stroked her head and as she looked up at him, she knew he had suspected all along that she was the bait.

She saw him go back to his room, heard him dress, and then he came back wearing his black ski suit and the Pierrot mask. He sat next to her on the bed and scribbled a note telling her that it was almost time for the night parade to go past the hotel, and that he would try to make his escape by mingling with the carnival procession. She was to join him at the last pavilion on Battlefields Park as soon as she could. She saw the pen linger briefly in his hand before he wrote, 'If the gods let us down, remember that I love you.'

And then he took back the slip of paper and was gone.

There was a sudden explosion of colour and music as the floats and bands of the night parade came past in a blast of trumpets, with revellers crowding and dancing around the floats, making merry on Caribou. She watched from the balcony, and could see him wait, his back to the wall, until the head of the parade had gone past.

He slipped swiftly away and mingled in the crowd, behind a group of massive figures, effigies of playing cards, and when she saw him move up between the Queen of Hearts and the Ace of Spades, she dared hope that he might be safe in this house of cards, that he'd get away.

But then in an instant a black-robed group swooped down on him like crows, surrounding him, obliterating him so that he disappeared from sight.

When the nuns drew apart and ran away, their robes flowing around them, soon to be lost in the carnival parade, Angela heard a woman scream. A circle formed around the prostrate body of a man who had just collapsed. Someone knelt beside him and put his head to the man's chest. He stood up again, shaking his head. Someone else threw something over the body. And then Angela saw it being dragged away quickly, hurriedly, from the parade, as if not to disturb the carnival festivities.

It was David's body and she knew that he was dead.

She sat cross-legged on the floor, the Pierrot doll on her lap, and much as she tried, she couldn't wipe the tears from his face.